WOLF
HONOR

ROCKY MOUNTAIN PACK

LUCÍA ASHTA

WOLF
HONOR

WOLF HONOR

ROCKY MOUNTAIN PACK BOOK THREE

LUCÍA ASHTA

Wolf Honor

Rocky Mountain Pack ~ Book Three

Cover design by Sanja Balan of Sanja's Covers

Editing by Ocean's Edge Editing

Proofreading by Geesey Editorial Services

For Mayu,
a generous friend with a beautiful heart.
♥
And for my daughters and beloved,
who laugh with me through this wild ride we call life.

A constant threat of death is good for one thing: to remind you to live the fuck out of life. No holds barred.

NAYA WOLF, HEIR TO CALLAN "THE OAK" MACLEOD'S WEREWOLF BLOODLINE

WOLF HONOR

CHAPTER ONE

CASSIA

THOUGH EVERY PART of her wanted to move, to thrash, to *rage*, the immortal stood still, only her chest heaving as she attempted to contain her ragged breaths and failed. Her nostrils flared, her forehead tightening with tension, her mouth a hard line.

But she had an audience.

And if the past thousand-plus years of living had taught her anything, it was that appearances were more important than truths.

Even if she couldn't see the bastard mage, Li Kāng, he was there.

He had to be. There was nowhere to go. No escape.

It was why she'd chosen Shèng Shān Monastery to stash one of her girls in the first place. The forbidding landscape was as much a sentry as any of the soldier vampires who'd monitored Meiling's movements for more than two decades.

The door of Meiling's chambers remained closed tightly behind them; the only other way out of the small, dim, stone room was a narrow window that opened to a drop of more than four-thousand feet that no mortal could survive.

Though the mage had been visible one moment and then vanished the next, Cassia was certain: Li Kāng was still in the tiny room with her.

Unless he could walk through walls...

Over the centuries, Cassia had met many magicians. Most were sad and ordinary, their powers limited to what amounted to parlor tricks. But there were always the select few who had extraordinary abilities. In thirteenth-century Turkey, she'd met a witch who could walk through any solid surface with as much ease as if she were strolling through the park for a touch of fresh air and sunshine.

Cassia's lips all but disappeared as she pressed them together until they hurt.

It couldn't be that. She'd have seen Li Kāng moving toward the wall before he phased through it. Her gaze had trailed his every move. One moment he stood beside Meiling's small bed, pinned in place like the scared prey he was, and the next he'd vanished, taking with him the storm of whipping clouds and wind he'd managed to summon when Cassia first entered the room. It wasn't every day she encountered a wizard capable of conjuring the forces of weather.

Swiveling slowly, she scanned the room. Her eyesight was as sharp as a soaring eagle's. If there was a shimmer to be detected, a distortion of the space around her, she'd spot it.

Her senses of smell and hearing were also pronounced, if nowhere near as strong as her sight. She should be able to pick out the man's scent and his breathing, which he'd no doubt be working to silence.

The white pepper that seemed to stick to every individual in the monastery, perhaps even to the walls themselves, clung to the space he'd last stood. It mixed with the scent of ozone she also associated with the mage, like that which preceded an electrical storm. That component of his signature odor had never made sense to her before. Now she understood perfectly.

"Grand Master" Ji-Hun had been holding out on her. She'd had no idea Li Kāng possessed this range of magic. The grand master vampire had only just escaped a brutal death at her hands when she'd accepted Master Xiong's offer to die in his stead. But now Cassia understood the extent of Ji-Hun's betrayal. He'd lost Meiling *and* he'd withheld information that affected her. Cassia might not have approved the mage as a choice for Meiling's immediate protector if she'd realized how powerful he really was.

Cassia *tsked*, thinking ahead to how she'd punish Li Kāng for playing this little game with her. She was all but certain the mage had to be responsible for the girl's disappearance—now and likely also before.

"I know you're in here, little fluffy bunny rabbit." She clasped her hands behind her back and began walking away from the door and toward the window. With how small the room was, it would take mere moments to bump into the man, who had to be hiding from her using invisibility magic—or a skill much like it.

She reached the window without discovering the mage and peered through it, wanting to stick her head outside to assure herself that the sheer cliff down was an impossible route of escape. But she wouldn't. Not when the move would leave her vulnerable to an attack from behind.

However, she saw enough to confirm that no one stood just outside the window. There was no ledge to perch upon. No place to hide.

She spun, hoping to throw the misbehaving mage off balance, but still heard nor saw nothing.

A few steps led her to the bed, little more than a dreary cot, placing her in the middle of Li Kāng's scent. It simply lingered from before, she decided, studying the thin mattress, yak fur blanket, and cold, damp wall behind them. No signs of the missing man.

Again, Cassia spun around, pacing the room until she reached the other wall and the small washing stand there. Another turn, another wall, and then another. Still no mage. No body.

Once more, her breath came too heavily, and though she wished to temper it, she didn't manage it.

Her lip curled as she spoke, scanning the empty room in all directions: "You won't be able to escape me. You're nothing. A small, insignificant challenge. I'll bite your head off, then spit out your fur."

She smiled as she envisioned herself already as a wolf, enjoying the hunt. Li Kāng was a rabbit with fluffy white fur and an even fluffier tail. So innocent, so pure.

She grinned, blinking away the vision. *Soon.* Soon enough that scenario would be real.

"Here, here, little rabbit," she cooed mockingly. "Come to me now. I won't hurt you." She laughed, surprised to hear it bubbling out of her like a giggle from the days before her father had turned her into the creature she was, when she'd still believed that life was happy and light, that good things happened often enough to overcome the bad.

"Come, fluffy rabbit. I promise I won't hurt you. Much."

Pressing her back against the door, she crouched to check under the bed. For an entire minute she watched and waited, surprising herself with her patience. But once more, nothing out of the ordinary gave away the mage's position.

Was there some other way the man could have escaped? And could that be why Meiling wasn't in here with him?

She'd ordered Li Kāng to not let her out of his sight. He should have obeyed. But the girl wasn't here. Had he stashed her somewhere? And if so, where? The monastery housed hundreds. It was a labyrinthine structure with an equal number of rooms, large and small. The girl could be nearly anywhere.

Cassia rose again and leaned against the door, crossing her arms in front of her chest, even kicking a foot back against the solid wood to sell the impression of her being relaxed. Of course, the mage would have to be a complete idiot to believe she wasn't fractions of a second away from murdering him. But in a life as long as hers, it was worthwhile to delight in making as many aspects of existence a performance as possible.

She stilled against the door, and then, without warning, lunged to the left, toward the empty corner of the room—

And snagged her prize.

Her fingers closed on fabric.

She tightened her grip, digging her fingernails into the flesh beneath, and was rewarded with a squeaky yelp.

"I caught you," she said in a singsong voice that even she recognized was a bit over-the-top dramatic. But it made her smile. "I told you there was no way to escape me."

Curling her hand into Li Kāng's top, she yanked him toward her with so much force that she felt him stumble—invisibly.

She dug her other hand into his shoulder and shook him as hard as she could. His teeth clanked as they smacked against each other. She hoped he'd broken some of them, and that it hurt.

Slowly, as if the mage were an image solidifying out of a staticky TV screen, his invisibility disappeared. Li Kāng stared back at her from a round, smooth face, nothing giving away his fear beyond eyes wider than normal.

For a few moments, neither of them said

anything as Cassia studied him, searching for signs she might have missed that would have told her of the abilities he'd kept secret from her.

Scowling at him, she shook her head in disappointment. And to think she'd actually liked him. Such a rarity for her to care whether a person lived or died, and for what? Only to discover once again that the one constant among the many people she'd known over the course of her life was that they consistently disappointed her.

"So you have invisibility magic, little *coniglio*, and you didn't tell me..."

Li Kāng's cheeks tightened, but he responded in no other way. That was as much a *yes* as she needed.

Cassia took half a step toward him so that her nose nearly touched his. Up close, it was easy to see how his eyeballs vibrated with the tension he was desperately attempting to conceal from her.

"What else are you hiding from me, hmmm? How did you hide your movements from me? I should have heard you at the very least."

The corner of one lip twitched.

"Ah. So this is part of your magic as well, is it? You can mask the sounds you make. What about your scent?"

Another slight twitch of the same lip.

"So it is part of your magic." Another time, she

shook her head. "And the power to influence the weather too, or at the very least to localize it. You have been a very busy bunny."

She smiled until she revealed both rows of sharp teeth. "And a lying one."

His eyes flicked to her mouth, and he gulped.

This close, she could more than feel his fear; she could smell it. Whatever magic he'd done to hide it before, he wasn't using it anymore.

"What shall I do with you now?" she mused, though of course she already knew she was going to kill him. A servant who didn't obey orders was far worse than not having one at all. He was dangerous.

She smiled somewhat dreamily at another image of herself as a sleek, muscular wolf who snapped the head off the rabbit in her strong jaws.

Then her smile dropped, and her eyes bore into his.

"Where's Meiling?"

He didn't answer.

"*Where is the girl?*"

Nothing.

"I see you're choosing torture before you die. That's more than fine by me. I'm in the mood to cause pain. You betrayed me. When I liked you. When I trusted you."

Only, truly, she'd never placed all her trust in

him. Grand Master Ji-Hun was supposed to have some of his minions keep an eye on Li Kāng while he watched Meiling.

For this, Cassia would be well within her right to punish the grand master for yet another failure.

When the mage still didn't say a word, Cassia shook him again. "Tell me where she is now and I'll let you off easy."

A lie, of course.

"I'll stop before gouging out your eyes and cutting out your tongue."

Li Kāng sniffed nervously but remained silent.

"Tell. Me."

When the mage still remained stalwart: "Fine. Then you leave me no choice but to make a spectacle of you. I can't have fools believing they can make a mockery of me and get away with it."

She dragged him toward the door, pulling it open. "You saw what I did to Master Xiong."

Li Kāng glanced back toward the room.

Cassia shook him. "*I said*, you saw what I did to Master Xiong, didn't you?"

Finally, "I did."

"Good. Then you'll easily be able to use that as a reference point. What I did to him is nothing compared to what I'll do to you. By the end, you'll be begging for me to end you. And I promise you, I won't stop until you tell me where Meiling is hiding."

"You won't find Meiling."

"Oh? And why's that? Are you doubting my ability to be"—she arched her brows—"persuasive?"

"Not in the least."

"Then?"

"No matter what you do to me, I won't tell you what you want to know. I've placed a spell on myself in anticipation of just such an event. You can torture me all you like and I still won't reveal what I know about Meiling."

Cassia's heart sped up, suddenly beating as quickly as if she'd just raced up Shèng Shān Mountain.

He dared trick her like this? Do this to *her*? After how good she'd been to him?

"You're lying," she said. "You'd say anything not to pay for your crimes."

"Not true." Li Kāng pointed his chin high and straightened his shoulders, even in her grip, making him as tall as she was. "I love Meiling. I love her with all my heart. For all the cruelty this place has tried to beat into me, nothing has been able to reach my feelings for her. Nothing will ever change that. I'll protect her with my dying breath."

He paused, then went on: "I knew you'd come

for her eventually. The way you kept track of her all the time made little sense to me at first. You delivered her here as an infant to protect her from those who would hunt her, so that she can carry on the werewolf bloodline that runs through her ancestry. That made sense only until I understood more of your true nature. I saw beyond your façade. You don't care about anyone but yourself."

Without blinking, he added, "There's no way you'd care whether werewolves eventually die out. Why would you? You leave a trail of death everywhere you go. You are the very kiss of death."

"Clever rabbit," Cassia said.

"It was only a matter of time until I figured out that the story you'd fed to Grand Master Ji-Hun couldn't be the whole picture."

"So Ji-Hun told you all this, did he?"

"No, he didn't. But we are all stuck on this mountain with each other. Eventually all things come to light. Like the fact that you entrusting the sacred book to the masters was payment for the maintenance of a single girl."

He snorted, seeming to build some courage. "That book is the only one of its kind. Sought by every scholar in the world. Powerful beyond measure to those who understand the importance of its messages. Someone like you would never hand it over unless Meiling were more valuable to you than the book. And what could possibly make her more valuable than the book that's at the center of the entire Seimei Do system? Or even beyond—of the Seimei Tamashii level of mastery?"

He tried to pull back a step, but she only tightened her hold. "No," he said. "It hasn't made sense to me for a long time. And then I found out that Meiling had a sister."

"How did you find that out?"

Cassia was composing a list of whom to kill. Her secrets were supposed to be valued above all others. Li Kāng shouldn't have been able to discover any of this!

The mage shrugged. "I listen when people don't notice. And the masters don't rely solely on the information you provide them."

Her nostrils flared anew. "They have spies? Surveilling me?"

Li Kāng shrugged again. "Perhaps. I don't know. But I learned of Meiling's sister."

"Where is Meiling now? Tell me and I'll reward you for pointing out those who've betrayed me."

"No one betrayed you. Because no one ever agreed to look out for you. You simply assumed everyone would since we all fear you."

Si, it should have worked. It always worked.

"I will not tell you where Meiling went, no matter what you say or what you do. No one on this mountaintop is more important to me than she is. I've made it so you cannot extract the knowledge from me. My spell cannot be broken by anyone, not even me. I did it that way intentionally."

Did that mean Meiling was no longer at the monastery? Even though Cassia had seen her and spoken with her not that long ago? Had she snuck past the guards and down the stairway again? She'd done it before, even when it seemed unlikely, or even impossible.

As if the mage had noticed his error as she had, he swallowed and said quickly, "Meiling is so well hidden within these walls that you'll never find her. And I'll never tell."

"You already said you wouldn't tell. And the rest are lies."

For a flash of an instant, panic flared across his face before he tempered it—then the impassive mask he attempted to hold in place was equally telling.

"The girl has escaped again," Cassia said.

"No, she hasn't. She—"

"Your desperation is clear across your face. Don't bother lying to me anymore."

He quieted, his shoulders drooping slightly beneath her grip.

She tried a different approach. "If you tell me where she's gone, I'll go easy on her. I'll still kill you, but at least she will live."

He hesitated. "I-I can't. I told you. My spell won't allow me to betray her."

"Only to betray me." Cassia allowed the full extent of her bitterness to charge her accusation.

"You never did anything to earn my loyalty."

Cassia temporarily lightened her grip, studying his face, especially his eyes, which told truths the mouth was unwilling to utter. She took in the defeated posture of his body, and yet how desperation ran just beneath the surface in a way that she could nearly touch.

The man was telling her the truth. He had cast a spell on himself. No matter what she did, she'd never gain the truth of Meiling from him.

The stupid fool.

He opened his mouth, but she didn't wait to hear what he'd say next. If it wasn't to tell her of Meiling's whereabouts, it would be useless—everyone but the three sisters left were useless to her. Now that Davina was dead and gone, they were the only ones capable of delivering the new life she needed to carve out within her eternity.

Without saying a word, Cassia slid her elegant fingers along Li Kāng's neck. As she began to squeeze, she knocked him to the floor, easily straddled him, then snapped his neck with a satisfying *crunnnchhh* that drew out, confirming that she'd entirely severed his spine from his neck. A crack along the skin of his neck widened and spread, filling with blood underneath.

Li Kāng's eyes were already blank.

Cassia scowled at him before finally rising. She had liked the man—at least before she realized how much he'd worked to undermine her.

She kicked him, hard. When it made her feel better, she kicked him another time, and then again.

"Why does everyone insist"—another whack—"on betraying me?" And a final kick. "And then they're surprised when I don't trust anyone."

She exhaled heavily, her gaze barely skimming the limp body on the floor at her feet. She tangled her fingers in the lengths of her hair and tugged, just to feel the pull against her scalp. To feel something other than the familiar, hollow disappointment.

"*Vaffanculo.*" A good *fuck you* was satisfying in any language. "*Vaffanculo*, Li Kāng. May you pay for your sins even in death."

Then she stalked out the door and down the long, dim hallway, unsure where she was going next.

She needed to find Meiling, and punish Ji-Hun in equal measure.

CHAPTER TWO

CASSIA

THE IMMORTAL'S tunic whipped behind her down the hallway. Her long, dark hair trailed her as well, weaving behind her in a perfect match to her internal agitation. She didn't even notice that her fury was riling up the air of the high mountains.

A young man approached from the opposite direction, dressed in those silly monotone robes the monks were made to wear. With his head partially shaven, a single tuft of hair braided, he looked utterly ridiculous.

The man pinned his gaze to the floor as his slippered feet quickly skimmed the trodden slabs of stone. She'd let him live for having the awareness to respect his superior.

He was an arm's length away, pressed nearly against the opposite wall of the passageway, hurrying to pass her. And then, at the last moment, he glanced up, looking straight at her. She caught the recognition in his astute eyes before he rapidly cast his sight back down to the floor.

She was unnerved, unsteady ... lacking her usual fortitude of a lioness, of a she-wolf...

He had seen through the crack in her armor—when it was her reputation for strength that allowed her to do as she wished with ease, to ensure she wasn't opposed by the other immortals.

As he passed, she spun around, her tunic and hair a graceful sheet as they swirled in her wake. She scowled, watching him scamper away. "You shouldn't have done that," she called after him.

The man's shoulders twitched, but he pretended not to realize she was addressing him.

"You *will* stop and address your elder instead of running away like a coward."

His step hitched, but he kept going, proving he was either more intelligent than she'd given him credit for, or far more stupid.

No, she decided. Had he been smart, he would have known never to look at her at all. It was his actions that had sealed his fate, not hers.

"Come here now, boy." Her command was a seductive snarl.

This time, the monk stopped walking, appearing

to quaver. Though his frame was strong, it vibrated with fear. She imagined she could scent it. When she was a wolf, she'd be able to.

"Did you catch my little display earlier, then?" she asked. "When I dispatched your Master Xiong?"

The monk's frame began openly shaking.

She couldn't decide whether or not to be disappointed that, after many years of rigorous martial arts training, this was the best the boy could do when confronted with a lethal threat.

Ach, it didn't matter.

She stalked toward him. The boy jumped every time her shoe scuffed one of the stones underfoot.

"Turn around."

The monk obeyed, seeming to have realized the inevitability of his predicament. He kept his gaze trained on the floor.

"You shouldn't have looked at me."

The boy bowed deeply. "I beg your forgiveness, Great Immortal. I meant not to, but then..."

"But then," she pressed when he hesitated.

"But then I couldn't resist your glory. You are a legend. Your power is spoken of in hushed whispers through our halls."

As well as anyone, Cassia understood the value of flattery. In the right circumstances, it was a useful —and highly persuasive—tool.

But she didn't think that's what the monk was doing. The timbre of his voice spoke of earnestness.

"And what did you see when you looked at me?" she asked, holding back from telling him that the answer to this question would seal his fate, one way or another.

"Ah." He cleared his throat, still staring down at his feet. "I saw ... I saw a being of such immense power that she seems as much like a god as any I've ever heard of. You hold the power of life and death in the palm of your hands. You have overcome death, the finality no one else can escape, not even our masters."

She chuckled despite herself. Ji-Hun was teaching the kids something of value after all.

"I do feel like a god." Not always, but much of the time.

The boy nodded, bent low.

"How will you tell of this encounter to your friends?" she asked, perking her senses to detect the truth in his answer.

"I will tell them that I had the privilege to exchange words with the great immortal." He paused. "And that she showed me mercy when she might have ended me instead."

The boy had been doing so well, and then he had to go and mention mercy. She was *not* merciful, nor could she afford to be considered such. People took advantage of compassion. They exploited it as the weakness it was. If the other immortals were to catch wind of her being merciful ... well, they might hunt her down and attempt to impose their will over hers. It had happened to others like her over the centuries.

It had happened to her father. Only he could never be blamed for mercy or compassion of any sort. He had underestimated her. And so, though he too had been an immortal, he roamed the earth no longer.

As if the boy sensed the gavel coming down on his fate, he added, "If you allow me to live, I will forever be your servant. I will use the rest of my life to spread word of your great power."

Cassia stared at him and that absurd braid that slunk down the back of his otherwise bald head, studying him. She believed him.

Faithful servants were always useful.

Finally, she snapped, "Very well! But do not think I am sparing your life out of mercy. I am doing it only because I could use a new spy to call on within these walls. That will now be you, understood?"

"Yes, thank you, Great Immortal. I understand and I accept."

The boy appeared to be somewhere between

sixteen years old and perhaps twenty-five. His bow was so reverent that he bent nearly in half.

"What's your name?" she asked.

"Bo."

"Bo, I need to find Meiling. Do you know who she is?"

"Yes, Great Immortal."

"And do you know where she is?"

"No, but I can look for her." He rose from his bow a few inches, though his eyes remained cast down.

"Do that," Cassia ordered. "If you discover any news of her whereabouts, you're to tell me immediately. If you can't find me, it is acceptable for you to tell my vampire servant, Édouard, instead."

"Of course. Right away. I can get out of my evening training."

"Good. Go now."

The boy bowed again, then rose and turned all in one motion, only glancing up when he was facing the opposite direction.

She called to his back. "And Bo?"

He waited.

"Tell no one of your role in my employ. Not even your masters."

Especially not the duplicitous Ji-Hun, she thought.

"As you command," Bo said, telling Cassia he was more astute than any of the vampires within the monastery walls. "Anything else, Great Immortal?"

"Not now. I'll seek you out whenever I need something."

"Thank you for the honor," the monk said, then walked away at a measured pace until he took a turn at the end of the hallway.

Cassia whirled back around, mollified. Things had a way of working out better than expected sometimes.

She took a right into another hallway, then called out to Édouard. Just once, and just loud enough that a vampire might hear her. As the mountaintop was teeming with the bloodsuckers, she tempered her tone so she wouldn't sound as desperate as she was.

Édouard found her when she emerged into one of the several open courtyards, the handful of her vampire minions in a group behind him.

Upon seeing her, Édouard offered her a subservient smile and bowed his head. "Mistress, I am at your service."

Five of the six vampires behind him bowed as well, elegant in their expensive suits. One did not show her the respect she deserved, standing stiffly instead.

She sought out his gaze, and when his eyes met

hers, whatever he saw there had him hurrying to bend.

"Too late," Cassia said around a smile that bared teeth. "Your respect for me isn't true, which means I have no further need for you."

He opened his mouth—to protest, presumably, but Cassia was on him in mere steps.

She wrapped both hands on either side of his head as his eyes widened in awareness.

His mouth gaping open, he squawked uselessly before she pressed her mouth to his.

His lips were soft and luscious, and she enjoyed the feel of them across hers as she sucked out every speck of his life force and added it to her own.

She was an immortal, yes. She didn't need to consume the life force of others to survive. But there was a vast difference between merely enduring and thriving. Every time she added the life force of another to her own, her energy levels spiked. Like taking a miraculous multivitamin, every life she absorbed made hers that much more delightful.

She licked her lips with relish as she released her servant's head. He crumpled at her feet, an unsightly withered husk.

Stepping over him, she faced Édouard and the others. Édouard alone managed to appear impassive.

The other, newer minions refused to meet her waiting stare.

Good. They'd learned their lesson, then.

She addressed Édouard only, ignoring the others, though she did have to swallow a smile when she noticed how one of them had to wipe the palms of his hands along his slacks, when vampires weren't supposed to sweat.

"The girl is missing again," Cassia hardly breathed. Though no one appeared to be near enough to eavesdrop, that didn't mean ears weren't trained on them.

Édouard's brow arched in question and surprise. "How?" he whispered, drawing closer to her now that he'd comprehended the severity of the situation.

Meiling was one remaining third of Cassia's chances to master wolf shifter magic. Should this set of sisters fail to meet her expectations, she'd have to wait another twenty-five years or so to repeat the process with a new set of desperate parents. She refused to wait that long.

"I don't know how yet, but it appears she's had the help of the mage all along."

News of Li Kāng's duplicity also surprised Édouard, whom Cassia never ceased watching closely to ensure his continued allegiance.

"The mage is dead now," she added, and

Édouard nodded. "But he believed her to have escaped the monastery already."

Édouard stepped even nearer, so that Cassia could smell his frigid skin. "Down the stairway again? What of the guards?"

"The mage's spells must be aiding her. It's the only way out of here."

"What would you have me do?"

"I will head down now to catch her. You inform Ji-Hun that he has betrayed me once more and to search the entire monastery, in case the mage has misled me again."

"And should I find her?"

Cassia's smile was as wicked as it perhaps had ever been. "Short of killing her, do whatever you have to do to make sure she's here waiting for me when I return."

"When will Mistress be leaving?"

"Now."

"Very well." Édouard bowed once more, spun on the other vampires working hard not to make it clear they were cowering behind him, and clapped his hands at them softly. "Come on. Make yourselves useful before our mistress decides to end you all for your incompetence."

As Cassia watched her most trusted servant lead

the others away, she wondered if she might someday call him a friend.

She shook off the thought and took the shortest route to the monastery's large, pompous front doors. Ji-Hun never left the place. She'd know right where to find him when she was ready to deal with him and all the ways he'd let her down.

With how little she truly knew of Li Kāng's abilities, it was possible he'd transferred his power to mask sight, sound, and smell to Meiling through some sort of spell. It'd be advanced, complicated magic, no doubt, but she was proof that the impossible was far less so than most people imagined.

Meiling had trained in martial arts as much as any other monk. She'd be light on her feet, quick, and stealthy. With the assistance of Li Kāng, she could skirt down the stairway right under the noses of a horde of vampire guards and they wouldn't realize it.

Arrogance. The greatest weakness of most vampires.

Cassia swept past monks still working to clear evidence of her earlier destruction, feeling many sets of eyes following her as she went. She emerged into the front entry courtyard and didn't even bother with the gates. Instead, she stopped feet away from them, closed her eyes briefly, and summoned the magic within the air around her that felt so similar to the immortality that pulsed through her veins.

The air was like her own personal life force: eternal, never-ending, tangible, and malleable in her eager and experienced hands. She wrapped the air around her as if it were a cloak, then she willed it to rise. As it did, she floated upward with it.

A few startled gasps reached her through the rushing wind. She welcomed them, knowing monks would recount how she flew until everyone else in the monastery knew of it. Until everyone there, not just Bo, thought of her as an untouchable god.

So that Ji-Hun and the vampire masters directly beneath him never forgot to whom they owed their reverence.

The wind whipped around her, muting any other sounds from the monastery as she rose higher. While she descended the mountain, she floated much more slowly than usual, inspecting the worn stone treads for any ripple in the air, any distortion that would suggest someone moved invisibly across them. Somewhere along those stairs, Meiling was hiding. All Cassia had to do was find her.

As Cassia gradually descended, she thought of all that was at stake.

Davina was dead. A brutal end to a failed experiment. There was no reviving the girl. She was a closed door. An investment with no return.

Meiling was on the run. A risk. An apparently uncontrollable asset. Cassia would have to force her immortality magic on her immediately to mitigate the risk of losing her again.

Lara, so stupidly fond of her forest and mountains that she'd never leave them, was exactly where she was supposed to be. She was the safest, so she'd go last.

And Naya...

Naya had also disappeared for a while, but she'd returned quickly. From what Maverick had told her, Naya seemed unaware that she was in danger within the boundaries of her pack. She'd bought into Cassia's fairy tale completely. She was no flight danger, not anymore. Not now that she understood immortals were looking for her. Thanks to how easily Cyrus had captured Meiling, Naya wouldn't be going anywhere anytime soon. Naya was almost certain to have heard of Meiling's predicament.

Even so, Naya would be next after Meiling. So long as Meiling knew where she was, and Cyrus knew of Naya's existence, even though he hadn't captured her, Cassia would have to contain the situation.

While continuing to scan the stairway on her

way down, the stationed guards failing to contain their awe at her as she passed them, Cassia pushed out her thoughts toward that familiar link.

The last time she'd tapped into Maverick, it had been when she'd learned that Naya was missing. But he'd told her they'd found the girl, suggesting the alpha was as competent as she'd hoped he'd be all those years ago when she'd selected him as guardian to her precious prize.

Cassia had done this many times before since imprinting a link between her and the alpha when she delivered a baby Naya to him.

She felt for his familiar energy. Gruff, strong, commanding—only he'd never command her.

Is Naya with you? Is she safe?

As if the immortal were speaking to the alpha in person, his answer arrived immediately.

Naya is with me, but she is broken.

CHAPTER THREE

BRUNO

AT THE FIRST sight of Naya collapsed across a tangle of tree roots, brambles, and stones, Bruno shed his wolf, running the final steps to her in his naked human form. But though Brother Wolf was back inside him, Bruno remained as intently aware of him as he was of the fact that, finally, he'd reached his mate—*he'd found her at last*—only to discover her *broken*.

Crushed.

Shattered.

Brother Wolf howled an equally broken lament, echoing throughout every part of Bruno's being in a mourning loop that might never end.

Bruno the man felt as if he could scarcely breathe. As if his heart might stop beating right then and there and never learn how to resume.

As if he'd never be able to erase this horrific image from his mind.

The full moon was continuing its gradual ascent above the mountain, illuminating the scene in a deathly pallor. Naya's wolf had overcome her while she was climbing down the back of the mountain. That much was evident. What was far less clear was why she'd attempt such a suicidal feat in the first place! Surely there must have been another option than this...

Than death.

His throat closed as he allowed himself the thought for the first time. Against all odds, he'd found his mate halfway across the world from the home of his pack, and now he'd lost her before even getting to tell her who she was to him—who he'd hoped with every part of him she'd get the chance to be.

Her thick gray fur was mottled, laced through with silver specks that shone in the moonlight. It would have been a magical experience for him to learn the markings of his mate's wolf for the first time ... if not for her silver specks being covered in thick blood that appeared black in the deepening night.

"She's not breathing," one of the other Rocky Mountain Pack wolves said. It wasn't Scooby. In that moment, Bruno couldn't recall the man's name. His focus was trained on Naya. Even his wolf senses that scanned his surroundings to anticipate threats had collapsed in on him. He had tunnel vision, only he had tunnel everything.

"You guys, she's not fucking *breathing*," the man repeated urgently, as if Bruno or Maverick could have missed that terrifying observation.

"We gotta do something. We've got to help her," the man added, and all Bruno did in response was gulp across a throat as tight as his tense muscles. They felt as if they were ready to snap from the pressure seething inside him.

Not only was Naya not breathing, but the impact of her fall had all but snapped her in half, bent as she was over a thick tree root. Her midsection was cracked open, exposing several of her ribs, a few of which were obviously broken.

One of her hind legs lay at an impossible angle, hanging loosely beneath flesh, though still attached to her body, and the one above it hung limply into the space the other one should have occupied.

A branch had pierced her neck from below, protruding above, a few bloodied leaves waving like morbid flags at the top. Bruno guessed there was a high chance the branch had punctured a vital artery.

Worse than even the pools of blood that reflected

the silver moon, her body was unmoving. No ragged, labored heaves through a punctured lung or two. No audible pumping of her heart. No whines or cries of pain beyond the first initial one that had caused Bruno to race to her like more than her own life depended on it.

Even after flying across the world to an entirely different continent, after tracking her to this remote location, he'd still arrived too late.

"I don't hear a pulse either," another of the pack wolves said, addressing the other man this time instead of bothering with Bruno, who looked as dazed and shocked as he felt.

"Alpha, what should we do?" the first man asked. "This is *Naya*. We need to save her. She's the *heir*."

Bruno growled at the shifter. He didn't care that she was an heir. They needed to save her because she was *his*. He needed her. He couldn't even think of confronting a lifetime without her, knowing what they might have shared.

"Alpha?" the man repeated.

Bruno hadn't bothered to look at Maverick since he'd spotted Naya. But now he turned toward him. Also returned to his human form, Maverick had crouched beside Naya's wolf, his hands pressed against his naked thighs. His gaze was unfocused and blank. Even his mouth hung partially open.

Normally, Maverick wore his intelligence and competence across his face, in the way he carried himself with confidence, with authority and power. Now he appeared nothing more than a vacuous shell.

"Maverick," Bruno snapped at him, and when the alpha didn't respond again, he shook him.

Maverick lost his balance and toppled backward with a hollow thud. He did nothing to catch himself.

His wolves scrambled over to him, but the alpha didn't so much as blink at them as he continued to stare—now up at the moon—without reaction.

"*Dude*, what the fuck's going on?" one of the pack wolves snarled, sounding ready to take on whatever assailed his alpha. Only whatever it was couldn't be beaten down the old-fashioned way.

"Mav," another wolf said, shaking the alpha by the shoulder.

Nothing.

So Bruno intervened, snapping out of his shock to take charge.

"You and you." He pointed at two of the three pack wolves who'd accompanied them to retrieve Naya. "Carry Maverick back to the plane. As fast as you can. I want us loaded and in the air as quickly as possible."

Wordlessly, the three shifters glanced back at

Naya, the remaining one sidling next to her as if to help Bruno shoulder her weight.

He shook his head. "I'll carry her alone. You watch our back. Your only job is to keep the rest of us safe while we make haste returning to the airstrip. You hear or see something, you even think you feel something out there, you warn us. Everyone got it?"

The three shifters nodded without complaint. They'd be feeling the authority of Bruno's alpha-level wolf.

"Now, let's move out."

All of them naked, the two shifters hefted Maverick up, linking their arms together to form a chair beneath him. Then they glanced back at Bruno, waiting for him to go first.

Bruno slid his arms beneath Naya's wolf body, forcing his emotions to remain under control. He had to focus.

"Snap that branch off from the tree," he told the lookout shifter. "I'm going to carry her with the wood in place."

He didn't explain why; the man would know. If Bruno were to remove it here, there was a chance she'd bleed out.

Assuming her heart would still pump.

That he could somehow revive her once they reached the plane.

Every sign indicated that it was too late, even for a werewolf. Even for a creature with advanced supernatural healing, she appeared too far gone.

But short of having their heads cut off, their hearts carved out, or their bloodstreams poisoned by silver, shifters could recover from the most advanced of injuries. Just because Naya no longer breathed and her pulse no longer beat, didn't mean he couldn't save her.

He *would* bring her back.

He just would.

Cradling her in his arms, he pressed her wolf against his bare chest, her blood trickling down his stomach and along his legs, sticky and unnerving.

He tucked her head against his shoulder, doing his best to adjust her body so as not to cause her more damage with his movement, but he had few options. Her broken ribs stuck out from her body like blades. He tucked her dangling hind legs in the crook of one elbow, draping her tail around them.

And after a final glance upward, at the dizzying heights from which she'd descended, shrouded in mist and impossibility, he took off running as fast as he dared.

With every step, she jostled in his hold. It didn't matter that his stride was light or that he was fast and agile. She was so damaged that each impact shook her in a way that couldn't be good.

But it was Bruno's only choice. He had to get her to safety. Away from the immortal who hunted her.

Only then would she truly have a chance at life again.

CHAPTER FOUR

CASSIA

"BASTARDI ARROGANTI," Cassia muttered to herself, startling yet another unsuspecting vampire, who actually squeaked when he spotted her—most unbecoming of a "guard." She couldn't believe she'd entrusted these buffoons to protect one of her prized experiments. No wonder Meiling kept escaping! The sentries were wholly lacking in imagination. It seemed they'd never seen anyone fly before, and so rarely looked up. If that traitor Li Kāng had indeed shared spells with the girl, then she'd likely tip-toed past the lot of them, who wouldn't expect her to be both invisible and lacking in scent and sound. Imagination was the death of power and agility; Cassia had plenty of it.

Seven-thousand-two-hundred-and-seventy-seven steps. That's what a shiny placard had proudly proclaimed at the top of Shèng Shān Monastery's grand stairway. What was *grand* was the size of Ji-Hun's ego, she thought with a ferocious scowl that spooked the next vampire on her way down. This one actually lost his footing when he noticed her, stumbling and nearly tumbling down the bajillion steps these master idiots insisted on.

Ordinarily, she flew up and down the steep incline without concern for the actual staircase that made it accessible to common people. Vampires, no matter how many centuries they'd lived, couldn't fly, a point that no doubt irked Grand Master Ji-Hun when he witnessed her traveling with her usual ease and grace. She smiled at the realization. At least *that* was something until she could get around to dismembering him in front of his adoring entourage. They'd soon see whom they'd actually been worshipping all these years.

Scanning each step for any sign that Meiling hid in plain sight among them dragged out Cassia's descent so much that she'd begun to fear the girl might actually get away from her another time.

She was a mere heartbeat away from punishing the guards for their failure to keep a single stupid girl in a monastery that had only one way out. *One exit!* Could it get any simpler than that?

"Incompetent," she snapped aloud. This time,

the nearby sentinel, dressed in a ridiculous maroon robe and thin slippers entirely unsuited for the high-mountain climate, didn't look up. At last one of them had anticipated her movements, but she was more than halfway down before any of them did.

She studied him as she also searched the area behind him for any subtle shift in the air. Gazes untuned to the air might miss a minor disturbance within it; she was certain she wouldn't. She'd spent too many centuries linking herself to the element. It would reveal any deceit folded within it.

This monk was young, as most of them were, his body strong and honed from endless hours of punishing training. At least Ji-Hun got that one thing right. Even though he'd deluded himself into thinking he was the chosen protector of the sacred book—or perhaps that was yet another artifice—the martial arts system he'd developed spit out ideal physical specimens ... on their way to supposed enlightenment.

She scoffed. There was no true enlightenment, or surely she would have found it in her thousand years of life. Somewhere, sometime, amid the impressive arcane and esoteric library she'd amassed, she would have found the key to it.

Though she stared at the monk, his hair in that hideous braid atop an otherwise shaven head, he didn't so much as sneak a glance her way. So he was intelligent as well as aware...

"What's your name, boy?"

This time, he did react to her, bowing low, still keeping his eyes away from hers. "It is Tai, Great Immortal."

"And how long have you been here at the monastery, Tai?"

"My parents brought me here when I was two years old, Great Immortal. They dedicated me to the service of the masters."

"And did your parents realize the masters are vampires?"

"As I never saw my parents again, I cannot be certain, Great Immortal." He hesitated. "But I do not believe so."

"Do you intend to become a vampire yourself when the opportunity is offered to you?"

Another hitch before Tai said, "I have not yet decided, Great Immortal."

Intelligent, aware, deferential, *and* wary of the creepy vampire masters. He'd make a good minion, better than the last batch she'd purchased at a premium price.

"If I invited you to leave this place and join me, what would you say?"

Beyond a jolt of tension that raced through his

bent spine, he didn't react. "I would say I am both honored and grateful to be of service to you, Great Immortal."

"Then when I return for Grand Master Ji-Hun—and I will—be ready to leave with me." She turned to continue her descent before reconsidering. "Gather a dozen others like you, interested in serving me, and they'll go with us when I come to retrieve you."

He bowed even lower, so that the one braid flipped upside down across his pate. The first thing she'd do was have them grow out their hair. In heavily accented English, he said, "With pleasure, Great Immortal."

Why hadn't she thought of it before? she wondered while she continued down the long stairs, searching every nook and cranny for a sign that Meiling was there. Already-disciplined minions were far better than untrained ones, and if she needed them to be vampires, that was easily enough arranged.

The musings kept her occupied until, three-quarters of the way down, through a gap in the dense foliage that surrounded the base of the mountain, silver light reflected off metal. She whipped around to find the moon already fully risen over a neighboring peak, now that the monastery no longer blocked her view of it.

Wherever Meiling was, the moon would be forcing the shift upon her.

As quickly as Cassia could without sacrificing the accuracy of her inspection, she sped down the steps. Even if the mage had given Meiling spells to use, from what Ji-Hun reported the girl had little control over her transformation. It was unlikely she'd be able to maintain the necessary focus to remain within the workings of any spell.

Even so, Cassia descended the remainder of the stairs backwards, floating above them, searching for anything out of place. Occasionally, she'd glance behind her. Though the guards, so far all vampires except for Tai, would be fools to try anything, she hadn't survived this long relying on assumptions.

She scanned, startled yet another sentry, who leaked urine through his robe and pants beneath, snarled at him for his cowardice, and caught yet another flash of metal shining through the tree canopy. She paused as she processed what she was looking at.

One plane belonged to the luxuriating vampire "masters," who taught an austerity they didn't practice. The other belonged to her. And the third?

There shouldn't be a third plane. There'd been only one other jet when hers landed.

Someone else had arrived since then. How had

she not heard it? As convenient as the invention was, its engines were unbearably loud. Perhaps it had landed at the time she'd been destroying Master Xiong and Ji-Hun's precious little throne room?

Wrapping the air around her tightly, Cassia flew so quickly that the air stung her face and caused her ears to ache deep inside her ear drums. How she'd missed the plane's arrival didn't matter. Neither did scouring the one exit from the monastery in search of an invisible girl. If there was another jet parked at the base of Shèng Shān Mountain, there was no way in blazing hell Cassia was going to let Meiling get anywhere near it.

She covered the final length of the stairs in a heartbeat compared to how long she'd taken to descend the previous stretches. All that mattered was getting the girl. She *would* become a wolf shifter and experience all magic had to offer her. Unlike so many others, she'd survived corrupt, putrid, and torturous circumstances for a very long millennium. She had earned the right.

When the ground drew near, a pained whine drifted through the trees. Cassia followed the sound like a hound on a scent.

A hundred feet later, Cassia found the girl.

Hunched over herself, her mouth poised open in a silent scream, her body lay broken and twisted and

LUCÍA ASHTA

contorted. Fur sprouted in small, barely there tufts across her bare skin, a pile of discarded clothing in a heap off to one side.

Mesmerized, Cassia categorized the order of the transformation. First, Meiling dropped to her hands and knees as her hips and shoulders broke apart. Then her head both shortened and elongated; her teeth grew. Her long blond hair shrank and morphed into thick, coarse fur, and her shifting chest spread to engulf her pointy breasts. A tail began to emerge from her tailbone, but it was only just a nub. Everything about the girl's shift was too slow and, apparently, also too painful.

The girl clearly didn't know what she was doing. Cassia would do it faster and better. She'd connect to her wolf in a way Meiling wasn't.

The immortal didn't bother to stem the grin that tightened her face. *Her wolf.* Now that she'd found the girl, she was one significant step closer to her goal.

A woman, also a wolf shifter from the way the moonlight reflected, making her eyes glow, broke free of the surrounding tree cover to rush to aid Meiling.

Cassia's grin dropped. The girl was *hers*. No one else was to touch her.

Moments later, two figures emerged from the shadows, momentarily stunning Cassia. She blinked at them, attempting to determine who—and *what* —they were.

Through their robes, hair, and long bearded faces, she could make out the mottled darkness of the trees behind them. The men were not truly men. They were ... translucent. Agog, she stared. They didn't appear to touch the ground, though from her vantage point it was difficult to confirm in the dim white light of the full moon. They seemed to hover and float more than walk, their gait too smooth, more of a glide.

Had they also mastered the air element? Would they match her skill in controlling it?

Though the shifter still hadn't noticed her, her attention fixed on Meiling, whose body was only fractionally closer to being that of a wolf, as one the two diaphanous men tipped their heads up to face her. Their eyes shone with the density of the forest, leaves and branches rustling within them, and yet their stares turned noticeably hard as both men shook out their hands and began mumbling rapid words.

Mages.

No mage should be anywhere near what was hers.

Now that they were turned toward her and she could easily study their faces, they were old. Wrinkles tugged at their sagging flesh, their beards and mustaches full and hoary. Even their bodies bowed subtly with the signs of age.

But their eyes held the strength of experience—and also the sparkle of excitement she'd only ever witnessed in youth.

As their lips raced through a spell of some sort, their shoulders rose in fierce determination.

Okay, then, Cassia thought. Not only would she fight for her property, but she'd *win*.

CHAPTER FIVE

CASSIA

SHE LOST track of Meiling and the progress of her shift as the two sorcerers, who bore sufficient resemblance to each other to indicate they must be brothers, chanted in Latin. At first, she paid attention to their words, attempting to deduce what kind of spell they might be crafting. They made mention of the darkness of night and the moon, the earth and the sky. But when they mentioned air, Cassia tuned out the rest of what they were saying, for when they mentioned her element, she sensed a tug along the length of her body.

The *stronzi* sorcerers were trying to wrest away her control of the air! No one could take away her link to the element—and yet they seemed capable of interfering with the bond she'd forged so long ago that she'd come to think of it as part of her very being.

But if the warlocks needed spells, then they weren't as powerful as she was. There were two of them, but she was the Kiss of Death. *Osculum Mortis*. Equally revered and feared wherever her reputation traveled. She was a fucking legend.

She clamped down with all her might on her connection to the air. Like a gauzy shroud, she sucked it in around her, pressing it to her body.

Their lips sped through their spell more quickly, more urgently, but they didn't panic when they had to have felt her pull away the control over *her* element they were so fervently building.

A whimpering moan that was part human, part animal, extended from Meiling. *Pathetic*. It was a good thing Cassia only needed the girls to be her test for the fusion of wolf and immortality magic and nothing else. *Weaklings*.

The other shifter, the woman, stood guard over Meiling, doing nothing but watching Cassia. At least the woman understood hers would be a wasted fight. Not even the two wizened sorcerers stood a chance against her. They'd realize it soon enough.

The air between Cassia and the men, cold in the deepening night, crackled like fire. The fine hairs along her body stood on end, electrified. To best concentrate her power, she lowered herself to the ground, visualized the air building between the palms of her hands like an electrical surge, and charged, rushing over the damp, slick, decaying leaves. Once Cassia slipped but caught herself, and then flung the air she'd amassed at the men.

The air hurtled toward them, and when it reached them, Cassia imagined it as a bomb. "*Boom,*" she said with a wicked smile as the wizards' long hair, separated into dozens of braids, flew back from their faces amid a racket of clanking beads. Their robes whisked backward, outlining their bodies beneath, slimmer than they at first appeared, gangly even, but Cassia's attack didn't diminish them.

Rushing to gather more concentrated air to throw at them, this time with the force of a tornado, Cassia steeled herself for their counterattack. She could feel it building to a crescendo; it had to be almost finished. The night itself seemed to vibrate with the intensity, and Cassia, who *never* went on the defensive, bent her knees slightly so that she could leap out of the way if she had to. But first, she'd let them think she was a stationary target.

Before she felt their attack launch, the first sorcerer yelled out, "Now! Your aim is true!" It took her a second to process the Latin she so infrequently heard spoken at her. When she ordered her legs to move her out of the way, she was too late. The mage's attack slapped her on the thigh as she bolted out of reach. As if by a giant hand, the impact was bruising.

Her mouth jumped open and she almost yelped, but she clamped her teeth down ferociously. When the worst of the sting passed, and her eyes were clear of pain, she whipped around to glare at them while also jetting out of the way.

And just in time. The second man launched his spell—exactly where she'd been standing.

The ground thundered and shook, taking the brunt of the impact. Again she was slapped, this time only against her heel. This attack hurt less, though it still stung.

Light on her feet, attempting not to reveal her readiness, she said on a dark chuckle, "Surely you don't think you can take *me* down with parlor tricks."

The sorcerers didn't answer.

She swallowed a scowl. They needed to speak to do magic; she didn't. On more than one occasion over the centuries, she'd managed to trick spellcasters into her taunts, sealing their deaths.

She tried another time. While she spoke, she sucked the air from all around her into her body. "All you have to do is hand over the girl and you can walk away." Her laugh was theatrical. "Or float, or whatever it is freaks like you actually do."

The men's eyes were unfocused as they took her

in, their mouths moving too quickly for her to pick up their words as they mumbled so softly she couldn't hear.

"Who are you, anyway?"

When again they didn't answer, she pivoted. "You're skilled. You've surely been around a long time to master magic like this. You must remember the old ways, when respect was always honored. When ladies and gentlemen fought after proper greetings and introductions." She paused. "You obviously know who I am or you wouldn't attack me without the courtesy of a conversation. At least tell me your names before I end your long lives. It's the right thing to do, or are you not gentlemen? Have you traded in modern crassness for the elegance of erudite society?"

Another time, they ignored her while they continued to chant their spells. So they were wise enough not to allow their emotional reactions to rule them. A shame. Knowledge was power, and true names were valuable in the magical world; they allowed for all sorts of supernatural attacks; the object of the spell didn't even need to be nearby.

Clenching her teeth at their impudence, she'd try a different tactic this time—and make them pay for their rudeness later. They were unexpectedly resilient to gale-force strikes. But would they be able to resist the magic that was uniquely hers?

"The girl is mine. I will never let you take her from me, so if you want to leave with your lives, hand her over now and I might forget you ever crossed me."

She wouldn't of course, but if they didn't realize that already, then that was on them.

The woman attempting to protect the *still* shifting Meiling snarled at Cassia. Again, Cassia grinned. For that, Cassia would kill her. She'd welcome the satisfaction.

Until then, Cassia had kept her attention on the greatest threat. She'd almost built enough force within her—

The mages charged her, zipping forward so quickly that she barely registered them until they were upon her, their gnarled hands cupping around either side of her face. Their power surged into her, and she felt stuck in their hold, magnetized to their grip burning her head. Any plan to defend herself, to disconnect from what they were doing to her, vanished in a wave of unimaginable heat, and the fear that she wouldn't escape whatever they were doing to her chilled her insides, even as her head heated to unbearable levels.

Her connection to the air dissipated beyond her

grasp. Her thoughts became foggy, groggy, sluggish, as if her mind might already be liquifying.

No way would her existence end this way. She was immortal. They simply couldn't kill her. No one who walked this world—or hovered over it—could kill her in any way but the one secret she alone kept.

As if they'd ripped off her head and punted it into a raging furnace, thought suddenly seemed impossible. She could no longer tell if she was holding in her torment. She hoped she wasn't revealing how much what they were doing was affecting her, but she couldn't be sure. Sound had vanished along with her ability to reason. Scents and every feeling other than that of her melting, dripping insides, were beyond her reach.

The element she always could count on had abandoned her. And the two fucking sorcerers, all ugly bushy gray hair and murky eyes, clouded what remained of her vision.

Her flesh began to actually dissolve and slide off her face. Incapable of jerking her hands up to touch her skin under the weight of the agony that held her in its thrall, of course she couldn't confirm it, but she was cooking alive as if inside a fucking kiln, she was certain of it—cracked and glazed and fucking incinerating. This was what cremation felt like.

Her lungs seized, her breathing halted entirely.

Their lips were still moving, she thought, though any time she tried to focus on any one thing, her sight blurred as if she were looking through a thick, hazy plastic sheet.

A violent pang twisted an organ in her lower right abdomen. Whatever it was squeezed like it was wringing the life out of itself, dividing her attention between the blinding pain in her head and her torso.

Next, a spike of pain swept through the length of her intestines, and she thought she might understand a bit what it felt like to be disemboweled.

Her heart thumped and beat frantically, as if it were attempting to rip free of her chest, causing her to gasp, drawing in an empty and wholly unsatisfying breath.

A sharp stab beneath her ribs. Another squeeze in the lower right.

Her throat ignited as if she'd ingested flames. She didn't dare swallow though she desperately wanted to. Anything to soothe some of the pain. Any of it.

Her insides were being ripped from her body. They had to be.

If she weren't an immortal, she wouldn't survive this. That much was certain.

She wished with all her might that she might be able to recede like a wave in the ocean away from all of it, to leave her body and its thousand discomforts for a while.

Perhaps she could will herself to die, at least for a short bit, enough for a reprieve and for these assholes to leave her alone.

They had to know they couldn't actually kill her this way, and that as soon as she recovered she'd make them pay, a thousand times over, for every torment they inflicted.

They'd get the kiss of death, but only after she'd practiced every single torture man, with his twisted, depraved mind, had invented over the centuries. They were translucent and therefore not entirely of this world? So what? *Cazzo*, she'd find the way to anchor them to this world before she made them wish for her to rip them from it. She'd make them *beg*, and wouldn't give them the mercy they desired as much as death.

Mercy was for cowards. For the weak. For the defeated.

Her entire form was pierced through with rough blades. All of it set on fire. Her every breath sucked from her chest before it could fuel her. Her heart was bloody and raw, her eyeballs burst pulp, and her flesh flayed from her bones.

She could no longer tell if the mages gripped her.

A flash of white-hot agony seared through what remained of her awareness.

If the sorcerers managed to knock her out, she'd be too vulnerable. Too open. They couldn't truly end her unless they drew out her immortality, and to do so they had to be immortals themselves.

But the men had already proven more worthy adversaries than anyone she'd confronted during a thousand years. No other way to end her should be possible. Immortality magic was so powerful that it was in a league of its own. Only that of its same kind could interfere with it in any way, draw it to itself.

Her father had once believed there was no way for him to die. He'd believed himself so clever, invulnerable, *eternal*—and still she'd ended him. If her father served any purpose other than to condemn her to a life she'd never asked for, it was for her to learn from his lessons. Hubris was the ultimate weakness. Arrogance was everyone's Achilles' heel.

If she succumbed to the suffering, allowing it to control her will, she might never wake again. Yes, chances were slim, and also yes, some days, when she didn't have to admit it to anyone but herself, she wished for a respite from all this living. But if she ever did leave this world, it would be on her terms, no one else's. If nothing else, she'd fought for that.

Her entire body had become one single open

wound that pulsed and beat and throbbed and screamed. Agony was all she could feel.

Her reasoning mind seemed to continue, as if on its own, but her thoughts were distant, as if someone else was having them for her. Certainly, with the state of her brain, she couldn't be doing the thinking.

With every ounce left of her will, she clung to remaining in her body. Whatever they did to her, she'd heal, and more quickly than any other supernatural creature out there. If wolf shifters recovered rapidly, then she was a hundred times faster. All she had to do was ... endure. Nothing else. Nothing more.

One wrenching, renting, ripping cramp at a time.

Just as she understood that every chance to save herself had moved far beyond her reach, a drunken, absent part of herself reached for the air, the one companion she believed she'd had—if not a friend, then at least a cordial acquaintance.

With the final shred of her will she could control, she released all the pain, all the parts of her that felt better once gone, and replaced the gaping holes with air.

She imagined it pushing out of her on all sides with the force of a tornado.

She had no idea whether anything actually happened or whether it all occurred within that distant part of her that continued to fight, to plan, to defend—until a sharp thud, a loud crack, and several whines and whimpers finally swam through her senses to reach her.

She sucked in her first full breath in what felt like an eternity.

At last, the pain began to recede. Too slowly, but it was going.

She didn't think she was on her feet anymore; she couldn't feel her lower body. Wherever she was, and however she was, there was nothing more she could do but hope the force of the air that burst out of her had been as strong as she'd imagined, and that she'd caused enough damage to those around her to give her immortality magic time to repair her.

It was the only way she was getting out of there.

CHAPTER SIX

CASSIA

LONGER THAN SHE should have waited, but not long enough to come close to completing her healing, she forced her body to move. Her parts still felt disconnected, each too invested in repairing itself, as if in her time of distress every piece of her had been cut off from the whole. Survival mode, something she hadn't experienced since her father was still alive, so many centuries before.

But that no longer mattered. Alertness was rapidly returning, and she was no longer at any risk of passing out and exposing herself to the wizards and whatever sorcery they possessed.

Eventually, she'd make them pay. *Oh, would she ever.* They'd experience every single agony she had, threefold. Translucent or not, she'd find the way, whatever it took. But now wasn't the time to provoke them. Not when she was weakened.

Opening her eyes, she blinked several times to clear the traces of haze from her vision. Still a bit blurry, but no worse than if she needed prescription glasses.

The sorcerers each floated up in the trees, bobbing just below thick canopies, as if that was all that kept them from floating up into the atmosphere. A vulnerability to keep in mind for when she got her revenge...

The wolf shifter who'd guarded Meiling was limp, unmoving, at the base of a large tree trunk. No apparent injuries marred her body.

And Meiling ... the stupid wench lay legs up, a quarter woman, the rest of the way wolf. Despite the fact that the moon had cleared the ridge surrounding them, casting the scene in silver, she hadn't completed her shift. Her torso was a mixture of fur and skin, her ears still partially human, her snout capped in a flesh-colored nose. The patch between her rear legs was more woman than wolf, though her teats were many and small. A single human toe stood out on one padded foot.

Like the others, she was unconscious.

Cassia scowled. She hoped she hadn't invested all these decades into producing idiotic, deformed werewolves. Her spies hadn't informed her of any issues, but perhaps Ji-Hun had simply kept Meiling's defects under wraps so he could keep the sacred book. It was all that ever seemed to matter to him.

Howls ripped through the night, and Cassia leapt into action. Or rather, she tried to. Her legs wobbled, her breath labored with every small step, and her head pounded as if it still remained clamped in an enormous vise. But ... she was moving.

Another wolf cry rang out.

Cassia stumbled over to Meiling's botched wolf, gripped her under the front legs, wrapped the air around them both with every ounce of determination that remained to her, and slowly, too gradually, lifted off into the sky.

Another howl announced the wolves were close.

Cassia clamped down on her connection to the air element, relaxed into it, and pictured it delivering her and Meiling to the other side of the clearing, where the trees on the other side of Shèng Shān Mountain were so thick nobody would spot them.

She knew from experience that her scent and Meiling's would rise into the air along with them, severing any trail a beast could follow. No matter how experienced a tracker they were, they'd hit a dead end.

Meiling hung heavily in Cassia's arms, dead

weight, but it wasn't actually the strength of Cassia's muscles that held her. The immortal's arms were cooked linguini. The air pressed Meiling to Cassia, carrying them above the trees.

Farther, farther, almost there ... and then they dipped out of sight.

Cassia trembled with tangible relief, willing the air to obey her commands and take them farther still.

When her mind felt like it shook with strain from directing the element, she let it go, and she and the partially shifted wolf plummeted to the ground, thirty feet below. The impact jarred every healing joint and rebuilding connection in her body, but Meiling didn't so much as twitch.

Bene.

She enjoyed the stillness for a few minutes, longer than she should have, before pulling out the mobile phone that allowed her only to text.

Have the girl. Begin your descent. Enemies at base of stairway. Message me when you are close to the bottom. She finished composing her message to Édouard, but before she could send, the telltale roar of engines powered to life. Her fingers still on the keys, she waited. Within five minutes, the mystery plane that parked next to hers on the vampires' runway flew low overhead, its nose pointed upward, gaining altitude.

Meiling's little sorcerer friends had left her behind...

Cassia smiled, and this time she felt her mouth actually respond to her emotions. Settling back into the support of a tree trunk, she waited for Meiling to wake up.

There was no need to push her body now that all threat was gone. Meiling was no match for her, and in her monstrous state she was a joke. One that was, lamentably, on Cassia.

If Meiling knew what was good for her, she'd wake the fuck up, finish her shift, and serve the purpose Cassia assigned to her. The only reason Meiling lived at all.

For if Meiling was of no use to her, well, she wouldn't have the chance to be of use to anyone else.

CHAPTER SEVEN

BRUNO

THE LOOKOUT ALTERNATED running at the back of their entourage and at the front, speeding up occasionally, scanning the landscape, only to drop behind to do the same. Maverick had trained them well.

Halfway back to the airstrip, Bruno heard Maverick tell the wolves to set him down. But even though the alpha was now clearly back in his body, Bruno didn't stop running.

Naya might be in Maverick's pack, but she was *his* responsibility.

And she wasn't dead. She couldn't be.

Bruno rounded a final bend, emerged from behind a thick copse of trees, only to slide to a stop.

He hesitated long enough for Maverick and the

other wolves to catch up to him, but then he took off again, aiming for Maverick's plane.

Whatever had happened in their absence had the wizards Mordecai and Albacus in frenzied agitation. The brothers waved their arms at each other while they debated heatedly. Cleo sat on the floor, hunched over herself, pale and seemingly sick. Another pack shifter stood beside her, his hands akimbo, staring with eyes narrowed off into the vast forest that spanned behind Shèng Shān Monastery.

Bruno couldn't be certain Meiling was at the heart of their distress, but he had a niggling feeling she was. Perhaps she'd simply run off, and they were concerned about having lost an out-of-control were-wolf in enemy territory...

Naya couldn't afford a single wasted moment looking for her twin.

Before Bruno even reached the jet, its engines roared to life.

Maverick. He must have commanded the pilot to prepare them for takeoff through the pack link—one of the many advantages of having a pack shifter as a pilot.

But as Bruno sped by the mages, one of them turned and called out to him in urgent desperation, "Meiling. The immortal took her."

"We tried to stop her—" the other brother added in an agitated rush.

"But she surprised us—"

"We attacked with everything we could put together in short time." The wizard shook his head with a tinkling clink of lament and a heavy frown. "It wasn't enough. She overpowered us. She's very strong."

"And sharp of tongue and wit. Even so, it won't happen again," the first one said, though neither of the mages appeared fully convinced, doubt and worry tugging at their jaws in identical fashion. "Now that we've faced her, we better know how to prepare for our next meeting."

"There was nothing we could do," Cleo told Maverick. "The mage dudes almost took her down, but then she sent out this fucking wild blast that knocked us all out for a few minutes, even them." She glanced at the wizards. "While we were out, the bitch took Meiling. Off into the forest we think, but we can't be sure." With a look at the other shifter whose name Bruno didn't remember, she added, "Davy didn't get here in time to see which way they went."

Beneath the jet, at the base of the extended stairs, Bruno stopped running. Waiting. But he wouldn't wait long, no matter what anyone said.

"We'll figure it out later," Maverick announced. "Everyone, up in the plane. Before she comes back and figures out Naya's here too."

The tension tightening Bruno's shoulders eased fractionally when the shifters and the wizards responded immediately. Davy and Cleo scooped up piles of discarded clothing, including Bruno's, and carried them over.

"Oh shit," Cleo uttered when she finally noticed the severity of the damage to Naya's body. "She looks bad."

"Up," Maverick snapped. "Everyone, up. Now. Go!"

They all raced up the stairs. Even the wizard brothers, whom Bruno had thought incapable of efficiency, floated up the stairway with haste.

In less than five minutes, they were all seated inside the plane, the stairs retracted, the doorway sealed, and the pilot rolling them forward, positioning them for takeoff on the short runway.

The engines groaned as the pilot pushed them to accelerate, and only once the wheels lifted from the ground did Bruno suck in a full breath. Only then did he notice he was still naked with Naya in his arms.

But he had no intention of releasing her. Not until he was sure she'd live.

"She's not breathing," Cleo whispered over what sounded like a strangled sob. "Shit. She's not fucking breathing." The woman's eyes glistened with moisture.

Bruno couldn't endure another exchange like this. "No, she's not. But she will. We need surgical supplies. I have to get this branch out of her neck and her chest closed up so she doesn't bleed out."

He was mindful not to allude to the obvious possibility that if her heart wasn't pumping, bleeding out might not happen.

The fact that it still might, however, was sufficient to prepare against it.

Naya wasn't an ordinary human. She was a werewolf. And Bruno was counting on his mate's nature to save her life.

"Right," Cleo said, nodding, visibly clearing herself of the shock that had taken Bruno far longer to shake off. The woman was tough as nails. "We have a serious first-aid kit on board. I'll get it."

"We'll have to at least wait until we're at cruising altitude to pull that stick out," Scooby said, sounding far sharper than Bruno had noticed from their earlier interactions. "It's gonna be tricky clamping and suturing in the air, but I can do it. Just give me the best chance at a steady ride."

Scooby glanced at Maverick for approval.

Maverick stared at Bruno for a few long seconds before nodding. "Do it," the alpha told Scooby, and the pack wolf immediately stood up, pushing up his sleeves as he moved through the cabin, presumably to wash up and prepare for surgery.

Mordecai and Albacus hovered over, and one of them said, "We can help with keeping the plane steady."

"That's right," the other said, and only after he stuck a hand in the pocket of his robe and clinked his runes together—a habit of his—was Bruno certain this was Mordecai. "We can stabilize the pocket of air around Naya and Scooby—"

"And me," Bruno grumbled, unwilling to temper the gruffness of his tone. "I'm not letting her go."

Mordecai smiled sympathetically through his bushy mustache and beard, his eyes mournful as if he were haunted by Meiling's absence. "Of course. We'll include you as well."

"Too bad we couldn't freeze the air the immortal was riding," Albacus snarled, appearing vicious to Bruno for the first time.

"Well, we didn't know she was capable of that," Mordecai said. "No one told us that part. How could we have known?"

"We still should have guessed that someone as

71

old as her might have mastered at least one of the elements."

"And what? Were we to prepare to defend against the misuse of every single element? And against her unknown type of magic as well? Be reasonable, brother."

"I am being reasonable. We should have at least anticipated the possibility."

"But we didn't," Mordecai said. "So all we can do now is prepare for our next encounter. Because there will be one."

"Guaranteed," Albacus bit out ferociously, and Bruno warmed to the eccentric mages even more. "She's ours."

"Definitely. She's not going to terrorize good people on our watch."

"Not a chance."

"Got the kit," Cleo announced, returning to them, busying herself spreading out the pertinent elements of said kit onto one of the beds, which was much like a massage table covered in a crisp sheet.

Scooby appeared behind her, hands held upright in front of his face in the universal way of surgeons whose hands had already been disinfected for a procedure. Only Scooby didn't wear gloves, a mask, or hair covering; they were shifters after all. Their systems were far more resilient than that of humans.

"Bring her over," Scooby said, and Bruno's wolf snarled without real reason.

But Scooby only chuckled. "I have a mate too. You can keep a hand on her at all times."

Still, Bruno hesitated until Maverick placed a hand on his bare shoulder. "Come on, man. You know you can trust us with her."

Bruno didn't think he'd be able to trust anyone else with her ever again. Not after she was as hurt as she was.

"The sooner I get in there," Scooby said, "the better chance we have at her coming back from this. Seconds count now, man. Be spright."

Bruno shouldn't have needed someone like Scooby—or anyone—to tell him this. But Brother Wolf was clutching onto Naya so tightly Bruno couldn't make him let go.

Mav squeezed his shoulder hard. "Let's go. Besides, I think we'd all appreciate you getting some clothes back on."

"Speak for yourself," Cleo said to a chorus of chuckles. "I'm enjoying the view."

Bruno couldn't understand how any of them could joke at a time like this. But he made himself stand up and lay Naya down on the makeshift surgical table as gently as if she were made of glass that was poised to shatter.

He ran a hand along her furry head, between her eyes, and down her muzzle while Scooby, the wizard brothers, and Cleo, who was going to serve as a surgical assistant, prepared to bring his mate back from the dead.

He closed his eyes and tried to pray, to connect to the lightness he felt so easily as it ran through the forest of his home in the Andes Mountains, where magic thrummed through every aspect of life so tangibly that he could very nearly touch it.

But all he saw was dark emptiness.

The perfect mirror of what his life would be like if he were forced to live without her.

CHAPTER EIGHT

MEILING

PANIC FLOODED her system like a jolt of adrenaline even as alertness was sluggish to arrive. Before Meiling registered the details of her environment, silver seared her neck, legs, and ribs. There was no confusing the painful sting that imitated prolonged exposure to a bare flame.

As a child under the tutelage of ruthless vampires, any of her minor rebellions had been dealt with swiftly—a silver collar designed exclusively for her, the only werewolf in the entire monastery— lucky her. Once, when she'd dared comment on the practice of local parents delivering their toddlers as offerings to the temple while ignorant that it was run by vampires who drank blood to survive, Grand Master Ji-Hun had himself fashioned a tonic laden with silver and forced her to drink it, relishing in the whimpers she had to swallow to get it down. She hadn't been able to drink or eat another thing for five miserable days while she'd waited for her insides to heal from the trauma—the one crippling vulnerability of an otherwise preternaturally enhanced healing system.

She could tell she was largely a wolf, but her mind continued to operate mostly as it did when she was in her human form. Sister Wolf was talking to her, but instead of being in control, she remained a passenger in her body.

For some reason, one that Meiling didn't figure had any chance of being good, her shift hadn't fully completed. Like a jigsaw puzzle, the final pieces were missing.

Every nerve ending fought the mixed results along with the silver. Her body could have actually been on fire and she might not have felt any differently.

Her breath was labored as she wrestled to assuage her alarm before it became one more problem to add to what was obviously a sizable list.

She was on a plane, that much was easy to deduce. The air was thin, the engines obnoxiously, almost painfully, loud. And every significant part of her body ached as it did after a particularly grueling sparring match, when she understood even before bowing her respect to her opponent that she'd bruise all over.

But what was worst of all was the realization that she wasn't on the plane Maverick had hired for their rescue of her sister. Though her sense of scent wasn't functioning optimally, she still registered the unique signature of vampires. For almost all of her twenty-two years, the scent of bitter herbs had surrounded her. Each bloodsucker's scent varied of course, but there was a tangible, pungent taste in the air that told her there was more than one of them on board.

And her newfound family didn't have any vampires on their team...

The evil immortal, however, did.

Meiling moved slowly, attempting complete silence, while she rolled her head around in the thick silver collar. Though she was clearly trapped in this tin can thousands of feet in the air, the door to the compartment someone had stashed her in remained open. She lay on thin carpeting, the floor beneath hard and cold. The walls were made of a beige plastic, but they could have been fashioned from pure silver for how much that mattered. She wasn't going anywhere on her own.

The metal at her throat had burned through fur to her skin. If she were able to look, she was sure she'd see bright, raw flesh. Soon, it would begin to blister.

Her front paws were linked together, as were her hind legs. And as if all that hadn't been enough to guarantee she'd be a docile mess intent only on surviving the pain, a double band of the metal hugged her rib cage like an elastic band. She kept her breaths shallow to avoid overly inflating her chest cavity.

Tears pricked at her eyeballs, and she furiously blinked them back, the ordinary movement awkward in a body that wasn't fully hers. Neither woman nor wolf, nothing felt right. Nothing felt easy.

An overwhelming hopelessness grabbed hold of her for several seconds before she managed to shake it.

Naya had an entire squad of fighters racing across the world to save her. She'd earned their love, their allegiance. And yes, Naya was heir to Callan "the Oak" MacLeod.

But so was she.

Even so, no one would be coming after Meiling. Other than Li Kāng, no one from the monastery would care whether she lived or died. Sure, she'd made a few friends over the years, bonding through the intense regimen the masters demanded they adhere to. But as much as they'd been friendly, they'd been competitors. The masters chose only so many acolytes each season to advance across the many levels of mastery. Meiling had always been one of the best among her peers.

No, her "friends" would be more relieved than concerned she was gone. She was one less person to beat to gain the masters' favor.

Li Kāng though ... her very soul quivered at the thought that she might never see him again. In all her time at the monastery, his had been the only genuine smile, his rare laughter reserved just for her. He alone had seen her as something more than one of hundreds of good little soldiers. He'd looked beyond her role as warrior monk to see *her*, and in doing so he'd been the one to show her there was so much more to her than a star pupil or a prodigy martial artist in training. He'd taught her that she was a girl first, and then later on a woman. That there was nothing wrong with being the sole werewolf amid vampires and the humans aiming to eventually become them.

He was a mage. She was a shifter. Together, they'd been the only two oddballs. Together, they'd made sense. They'd matched. Balanced each other.

And he'd given her so much hope. Suggested she dream of a life outside of the monastery walls, where anything was possible. Where she wasn't obligated to fulfill the wishes and whims of ancient vampires, and where she didn't need to tiptoe around hoping they wouldn't notice her.

A fresh wave of tears stung her eyeballs, the one part that hadn't hurt.

She was alone. The only person who believed in her might as well be an entire universe away.

The same with her newfound sisters.

Meiling froze, and the tears retreated.

If she was on Cassia's plane, then it was possible that Naya was on board with her. Wasn't it?

Naya had taken Meiling's place in the monastery. It was unlikely her sister had managed to escape.

Did Cassia have both of them? The consideration was too terrifying to provide any relief. Naya's existence might be a recent discovery, but she was family that Meiling had never believed she had. She'd protect any of her sisters at all costs.

"Mistress," a man called from nearby. "The girl is awake."

Meiling barely breathed while she waited.

"Took long enough, didn't it?"

Her heart squeezed as she recognized the unmistakable lack of compassion in the immortal's voice. Beneath that smooth, seductive roll, there was no mistaking the calculating power.

"Well?" Cassia pressed of the man. "Don't make me drag the answers out of you, Édouard. Has she finished her shift yet or not?"

"No, Mistress, she hasn't. She doesn't appear to have progressed at all from when you last saw her."

A perilous silence. "She does nothing but disappoint me."

Then take the silver off, sāobī, *and see what happens then.* Obviously Meiling couldn't complete her shift like this!

Cassia's heavy, put-out sigh still somehow managed to remain elegant, before she added, "At least she won't disappoint me for much longer. I'll have all I need from her soon. I won't need to concern myself with her anymore."

There could only be one reason for her lack of interest. It wasn't like Cassia was the kind of bitch to allow her prisoners to just leave.

"Come, Éd," Cassia went on. "We'll go over my scientists' findings again. When we land, I want us ready to move on the merge immediately. The longer the girl remains alive, the more she inconveniences me."

As Édouard scurried off to do the immortal's bidding, Meiling stared blankly up at a curved plastic ceiling.

Cassia was going to chew her up, spit her out,

then flush her down a toilet. She was going to kill her and not so much as bat an eyelash in remorse.

No one was coming to Meiling's rescue.

If she was going to survive, it was all on her to find the way.

Despite her visceral dislike of the vampire masters, they had done one thing right. They'd crafted her into a formidable weapon.

All she had to do was bide her time and wait for her chance. The very instant she got it, she was taking it. And she was going to make it count.

CHAPTER NINE

BRUNO

HE DIDN'T LEAVE Naya's side while Scooby removed the branch from her artery, snapped her ribs and hind legs back into place, and sewed up her gaping midsection. Even while Cleo had disinfected the other many scrapes and cuts that littered Naya's body, Bruno didn't move.

But after an hour passed and Naya still hadn't sucked in a breath, her heart still hadn't thumped—not even once—Bruno couldn't think. All he could do was feel, and feeling was too much right then. So he did what he hadn't thought he'd be able to do, and he left Naya with Cleo, who held his mate's paw with a tenderness that assured his Brother Wolf that the women were friends, and that Cleo wouldn't let anything happen to Naya while he was gone.

The plane was equipped with a shower, and

Bruno washed Naya's blood from his body, hoping with every beat of his heart that it wouldn't be the last time he felt her on his bare skin.

Clean and dressed, he positioned himself at the head of the bed, where he could stare at Naya's wolf's face. He pictured her eyes opening and staring back into his so hard that he figured, if he possessed any magic at all, it'd be strong enough to will his imaginings into reality.

But nothing happened. She continued to lie limp, lifeless, her body battered and seemingly injured beyond repair, even for a werewolf with preternatural healing.

"How far do you figure she fell?" Bruno asked Maverick softly.

The alpha had rarely left Naya's side, and when he did, it was only to organize his pack. He'd ordered the second assault team to turn around in mid-air when they were approaching Shèng Shān Mountain.

Maverick ran a hand across his tired face before leaning back into his seat with a burdened sigh. "I don't know, but I'm guessing maybe a couple hundred feet. I dunno, maybe less. Still, it's incredible that she made it down as far as she did. That rock face..."

"Was a beast," Scooby added in, coming over to check on his patient. "I didn't think anybody could climb down that. That shit was crazier than El Capitán."

"It was like El Capitán's big, scary-as-fuck, badass big brother," Cleo said, also referencing the famous climbing route in Yosemite Valley that was braved only by the most experienced of climbers—and, at times, claimed their lives.

"Naya's nuts, dude," Scooby said, but Bruno calmed his wolf's immediate defensive reaction when he heard the fondness in the man's voice. "No one else would've attempted that climb, not even Howie or Jeb."

Silence for a few seconds. The air in the cabin was as heavy as their spirits.

Then, Cleo whispered to Naya, "Come on, girl. You gotta pull through this. You can't let that twat of an immortal take you down. You're a legend."

And so was Cassia, Bruno thought bitterly.

As if Maverick's thoughts had also turned to the immortal, and then her latest kidnap victim, he muttered, "I'd been hoping to track Meiling with Naya's wolf-head pendant again, but it hasn't moved from the airstrip. The necklace must've fallen off when Meiling shifted."

"Probably," Cleo said, just as glumly. "Meiling was really upset about Naya when the shift came over her. I think she thought she had more time before the moon did its thing." After a pause: "We've got to get her back. Naya would want us to."

Maverick pursed his lips. "Remember who's the alpha here, Cleo," he said, pulsing authority into his statement, but no anger.

"Right. Sorry, Mav."

Maverick smiled softly at her, as if he'd only told her that because he knew an alpha should, and for the first time Bruno saw him as a father figure to his pack wolves.

"I'll do my best to get her back. But Naya comes first. She's my priority."

At least on that point Bruno could readily agree. He liked Meiling just fine. He enjoyed her company; he was eager to learn more about the martial arts she'd been taught as an acolyte within the walls of the vampire monastery. And he very much wanted to free her from the immortal's control; no one should be abandoned to that fate.

But she wasn't his mate. She wasn't the one his Brother Wolf needed to protect at all costs.

"Once Naya's home and safe," Maverick added, "I'll figure out what we can do to get Meiling back. We're going to need to regroup and come up with a solid plan before we take on Cassia."

Together, Bruno, Maverick, and Cleo glanced up

at Naya, spread out on the makeshift medical bed on her side, just as Bruno had found her.

Gently, Cleo asked, "Why isn't she waking up? No matter how far she fell, that alone shouldn't be able to kill her." She hesitated. "Right?"

As much as Bruno longed to deny it, the evidence was continually suggesting that it might indeed be possible. Every breath and beat that Naya's body skipped enforced the terrifying possibility.

Bruno had seen many dead wolves over his lifetime. Hunters pursued wolf shifters all over the world with a single-minded goal: to eliminate them simply for being what they were, a nature they were powerless to change. Naya looked just like those wolves, so utterly and wholly unmoving. She *felt* like those dead wolves. As if the magic that animated her had already fled her body.

Bruno jumped out of his seat. "We have to try something else. We have to do something. Now."

Desperately, he searched the cabin, looking for some idea of what they could do. What else they could try.

Werewolves were slightly less resilient than wolf shifters, but their ability to survive what would be impossible for their human counterparts was consistent.

Naya still had her heart and her head, and no silver poisoned her system. There *had* to be a way to jumpstart her return.

"Scooby," he called, stalking over to where the man was just returning to his seat, appearing exhausted, weighed down with concern for his patient.

"What's up?"

"Are you sure her lung isn't punctured?"

"I'm sure. I had a good look; her whole ribcage was busted open. Both her lungs are working properly." He grimaced. "Well, they would be—they should be—if she were breathing, ya know."

Bruno forced his thoughts beyond the panic that hadn't let up for a moment since he'd first spotted Naya's lifeless form sprawled out beneath the silver moonlight.

He made himself continue. "Okay. So I know we don't have a defibrillator on board"—it was one of the first things Scooby had lamented once he'd started operating on Naya—"but is there something else like it that we could use?"

"Naw, man. I told you, we don't have anything like it here because we don't ever need it. You know what it's like. Wolves either recover on their own ... or they don't. With Naya patched up like she is, she has a ... a good chance at coming through this."

But Scooby's eyes, usually vivacious, were devoid of the hope Bruno needed to feel.

"And before you ask, no point in doing CPR either, or I would've done it when I first saw her. Her heart's gonna have to beat on its own. It's what her body's made to do."

When Bruno didn't look convinced, Scooby added, "I'd potentially cause more damage to her ribs if I tried to push down anywhere near them. She's too broken for that."

"She's too broken not to do everything in our power to help her," Bruno said in a low, gruff voice that barely managed to contain his inner turbulence.

"I know, man, I know, but there's nothing left to do. We just have to wait and see what happens."

"Do I look like I can just wait and see?"

Scooby stared up at him before sighing. "No, you sure as shit don't. But for real, dude, if there were a single thing I could think of to help her, I'd've done it already. Twice over. We don't carry things like adrenaline injections because it's not something we ever have need of. If she were poisoned, I'd have things to do. But she's just plain hurt. Our only option is to wait."

Bruno stared back at Scooby until his eyes lost focus. Then he turned, searching the cabin again, his attention landing on the wizard brothers. They were awake, hovering just above the floor in seated positions next to the open space by the exit door, leaning over to study Mordecai's runes. The small stones lay in haphazard fashion beside them, their foreign, unintelligible markings seeming to tell the brothers a story of some sort. They were engaged in a hushed yet heated conversation.

Without turning back to face him, Bruno asked Scooby, "What if they could use magic to shock her heart back into beating?"

Scooby leaned around Bruno to check out the wizards. "Like a mage-fueled defibrillator?" He paused. "Yeah, that might work. I mean, if something like that is gonna work, and there's no guarantee. Naya's heart is fully capable of starting back up on its own."

But Bruno had already heard everything he needed. When he crouched in front of the wizards, Maverick and Scooby were already moving toward them.

"What do the runes say?" Bruno asked the mages.

Mordecai scooped up his stones, sliding them into a small, worn velvet bag, before stuffing it into the pocket of his robe. "To listen to you right now."

Bruno nodded. "What kind of magic can you do?"

"Oh," Albacus said, surprised. "Quite a lot at this point. We've been fascinated with the study of magic since we were wee ones growing up in the palace of Irele."

"Irele? I haven't heard of it. Is that in France?"

Visibly blinking away troubled thoughts, Mordecai chuckled. "Heavens no. Irele is deep in the English countryside. Whatever gave you the impression it would be in France of all places?" He screwed up his features as if Bruno were the silliest man to come along in a good while.

Bruno felt his forehead scrunch. "I thought you were French, so I assumed you'd grown up in France ... or perhaps one of the other French-speaking regions of the world."

Mordecai chuckled again, sounding far too tickled given the circumstances, entirely child-like in his ability to be present for whatever was happening in the moment. "What an odd thing to think."

"Perhaps not, brother. Remember how many places we've visited over the centuries. Our mannerisms might be perplexing to someone who's only lived a short time in comparison."

"You were speaking French," Bruno said in an even, deadpan tone.

"Oh," Albacus said again, and then both brothers threw their heads back in hearty laughter, a symphony added to by the tinkling of the myriad beads adorning their hair.

"We were speaking French," Mordecai finally wheezed out.

Albacus opened his mouth to add something, but couldn't get it out over his laughter.

"What are we missing here?" Maverick snapped from where he towered over the seated men.

The alpha's stern tone did nothing to dampen the brothers' delight, however. After another half minute, their mirth fell from their faces—while continuing to twinkle across their light eyes.

"We speak French because we love it," Albacus said in the way one would express an overtly obvious fact. He smiled again. "Such a melodic, rich language. In the parlance of the times, *duh*."

Bruno swallowed and forced himself to wait this out. Hadn't Boone warned them that this was just how the brothers were? Patience was key with them, especially when Bruno was about to ask them to use their powers.

Albacus elbowed Mordecai. "My brother here has an infatuation with a certain beautiful witch, and she *is* French."

Mordecai scowled at his brother. "I am not infatuated with Arianne. She is far too magnificent for something as mundane as"—his mustache curled along with his lip—"infatuation."

"She's the reason for your sudden great love of French, is she not?" Albacus pressed.

"Sudden? Brother, I think even for us *sudden* cannot refer to someone we met more than a century before."

Annnd that was the end of Bruno's patience. Not that he wasn't curious about these men and the apparently highly peculiar lives they led, but—

"What kind of magic can you do?" Bruno asked. "Please. I want to know if you can help save Naya's life."

"Ah," Albacus said as if Bruno's intent hadn't been at all apparent.

From behind Bruno, Maverick grumbled something under his breath that sounded a lot like "...these guys should come with a warning label."

"Well," Albacus started. "We can extend our lives beyond the usual life expectancy, obviously."

"And we can each maintain a half-life, sharing each other's life force," Mordecai added.

Albacus brought up a hand with gnarled knuckles, the wide sleeve of his robe gaping open to reveal pale skin that looked like it never saw the sun. He ticked off on his fingers. "We can portal travel, preserve memories in objects, animate the inanimate—"

Mordecai jumped in. "Break most curses, depending on their severity; create a bridge to other dimensions for parlance; and change a person's appearance, temporarily at least."

"We can—"

"I see that you are quite skilled," Bruno interjected. "I should have asked a more specific question."

Albacus smiled gently. "Always a good idea with us, I think. Or should I say, *je pense.*"

Another round of child-like giggles swept across the two men before they quieted on their own this time.

After tugging on his long beard as a businessman might arrange his tie, Mordecai asked, "What is it that the runes guide us to hear?"

Bruno had no idea what the runes wanted, but he knew what he needed. "Can you jumpstart Naya's heart? Maybe her lungs too?"

The wizards turned to look at each other, wearing perfectly matching expressions: bushy eyebrows raised, eyes wide, mustaches twitching.

They turned back to Bruno at the same moment.

"We can," Mordecai said.

"Or at least," Albacus added, "we have abilities we might be able to adjust to suit that purpose."

Bruno glanced up at Maverick. The alpha appeared as hopeful as Bruno suddenly felt.

"Let's move," Maverick said. And to the wizards, "What do you need us to do?"

Mordecai waggled his mouth back and forth, appearing pensive. "Give us a hand up?"

Without hesitation, Bruno and Maverick reached to help the wizards.

Their hands slipped through the mages' grips as if the wizened men consisted of water. An electric shock zipped up Bruno's arm, and he hastened to pull it away, shaking out his hand. Maverick was doing the same.

"Sorry," Mordecai said, the mischief in his gaze suggesting he was no such thing. "Couldn't resist."

The brothers stood on their own, far more limber than Bruno would have guessed given how ancient they were.

And as the mages swept past them toward Naya, Albacus called over his shoulder, "You guys are such fun."

More unsettled than he was before, Bruno raced after the wizards, ready to forgive them their every eccentricity if they would just bring his mate back to him.

CHAPTER TEN

BRUNO

BRUNO, along with the half-dozen pack wolves in the jet's cabin, gathered around the medical bed where Naya lay.

"Give us some space, folks," Mordecai said, spreading his arms wide to encourage them to move back, his robe draping as if the man had dark wings.

"Worse than the crowds that used to gather for witch burnings," Albacus muttered. "Pressing in on all sides, barely letting you breathe. Do you remember how bloodthirsty those poor misguided souls were? Wanting to gape at the suffering of others?"

Mordecai grimaced. "How could I ever forget?"

Bruno scowled at the brothers but didn't voice his complaint. Never had he met a pair worse at reading the mood of a room. The wizards definitely floated along life to their own shared tune.

"Do you think it'll work?" Maverick asked them. He and Bruno were the only ones not to step back at the mages' request.

"We wouldn't be giving it a whirl if we didn't think it has a good chance of working," Albacus said, waving both arms in what seemed like a senseless flourish.

"Not entirely true, brother," Mordecai said. "I think we'd do it either way. New problems to solve, new ways to apply our magic—"

"Always such a joy." Albacus tilted his face upward as if he were imagining a perfect, sunlit day.

"What exactly are you going to do?" Bruno asked, suddenly wary. "There's no risk that what you'll do will hurt her, is there?"

Albacus and Mordecai both squared to face him. Albacus raised a brow, while Mordecai said, "It appears we've reached the stage where the risks of what we're to do don't much matter. It's worth any opportunity to bring her back, wouldn't you say?"

Yes, Bruno would say that, but the word lodged in his throat. The thought of anything further hurting Naya was unbearable. But the wizards were right.

"Do whatever you need to do," Maverick said. "Just bring her back to us."

"Oh, no, no, no," Albacus said. "Not like that. We won't be bringing her back from the dead. If she's well and truly gone from this plane, she'll stay that way. We won't have anything to do with reviving someone who's already moved on from this world."

Mordecai crossed his arms over his chest, as if the matter were actually in question. "That's right. We might be fascinated by magic of all types, but don't mistake us for necromancers. That is one line we won't cross."

"Ever," Albacus added.

"Ever," Mordecai echoed. "There are few natural laws better not messed with, but that is one of them. The dead should remain dead."

"They're never the same once they're revived."

"Never."

"Always best to leave the dead as they are," Albacus added, appearing ready to continue the moot discussion.

"We aren't asking you to bring her back from the dead," Bruno interrupted, working hard to keep the snarl from his voice. He needed the oddballs ready and eager to help Naya. "Naya is still here with us. She just needs a little help."

As one, the group swiveled to study Naya.

Dios mío, she does look dead, Bruno thought before he could stop himself. It became difficult to breathe, but he pushed on, pinning the brothers in a hard, determined stare. "Do everything you can. Help her return to this life while she still has it."

Maverick growled, and Bruno understood that his alpha wolf didn't appreciate that Bruno was giving orders. Tough luck. Bruno no longer cared about the rules of hierarchy among wolf packs. He cared about one thing only.

He leaned his hands to either side of Naya, his jaw hard, his heart beating too quickly as if to also beat for his mate beneath him.

"Do it. Now. Please."

The brothers stared at him for a few moments before Albacus smiled sympathetically, his gaze dreamy for a moment. "Young love. Like nothing else in this life. And now I barely remember what it felt like..."

Mordecai rested a hand on his brother's shoulder as easily as if they were fully solid. "Do you want to start us off?" he asked softly, seeming to hope to steer his brother away from some painful memories.

Albacus nodded his head sharply to clear it, setting dozens of beads to chiming as they knocked into each other. "Yes, yes. Definitely. The spell for lightning, I think, don't you?"

"To start. Too bad Clara isn't here."

"Who's Clara?" Maverick asked.

"Only the best intuitive witch we know," Mordecai said. "For all our centuries of training—and I won't be humble here, it won't serve any of us—my brother and I are as skilled as they come—"

"But we can't do what Clara can," Albacus said. "Not without spells."

"No one can."

"Can we find this Clara?" Bruno asked. "Can we pick her up?" He looked at Maverick, silently asking the alpha if they could reroute the plane, refuel if needed, and get this miraculous-sounding witch so she could fix Naya already.

"Clara is out of reach," Albacus said with a heaviness that suggested he hadn't seen this Clara in too long. "But we'll do nicely enough."

"We do know what we're doing, you know." Mordecai added an admonishing look, as though Bruno were the one suggesting someone else would be better suited to the job.

"We are considered by many to be the best in the entire magical community," Mordecai said. "Not to toot our own horns."

"Toot," Albacus said, sounding remarkably much like a bicycle horn. He must've practiced.

"Simply to put you at ease. We might go about things the roundabout way—"

"But we get the job done."

"Prove it," Maverick growled while Bruno worked very hard not to voice his own opinion of how long all of this was taking. Every minute that ticked by and Naya didn't draw breath dug away at the fragile hope Bruno was holding on to like a life raft in a vicious ocean storm.

"It's a good thing Sir Lancelot isn't here," Mordecai said under his breath to Albacus, "or he'd be having a fit about manners."

"I can almost hear him now," Albacus said over an affectionate chuckle, but at least the translucent mages were moving now, positioning themselves, one at the head of the bed and one at the foot.

They spread their arms wide, and closed their eyes. A moment later, Albacus opened one, glaring at Bruno and Maverick. "Back. Out of the way. Or we might end up killing you."

Even so, Bruno and Maverick both growled and took their time stepping away. For Bruno, it was like fighting the draw of a powerful magnet.

He needed to be near Naya.

But he needed to survive to share a life with her more.

Come on, Naya, he whispered through his thoughts. *You can do this. Come back to me.*

Then the mages began chanting in Latin. Though Bruno had never studied the archaic language, he spoke several Romance languages. That alone was enough for him to pick up on the gist of what they were saying.

For the first time, he feared their intentions. Not because either of them seemed inclined toward dark magic, but because of what was at risk. He'd placed the fate of the woman he loved in the translucent hands of two men he barely knew, but who were undoubtedly capable of great feats of magic. They could do whatever they wanted to Naya now and there wouldn't be much Bruno could do to stop them.

But this trust was necessary, Bruno reminded himself. And Boone trusted the wizards completely. Bruno had instantly liked the beta of the North-western Pack and had faith in his judgment.

Tension rode every muscle in Bruno's body. He squeezed his thighs and then his arms with his hands just to give him something to do. Every instinct racing through his body, through Brother Wolf, urged him onward to interfere, to do whatever necessary to save Naya himself.

But Naya was beyond his saving.

The chanting rose in volume, and the energy surrounding them began to vibrate, charging with unseen force.

Several times, Bruno heard the brothers chant

variations of the Latin word *lux*. Light. The lightning they'd mentioned.

They were summoning the power of lightning! Inside a flying jet with electrical controls.

Would the old wizards who'd been born in a time well before electricity take into account the fact that, if their magic created an event similar to an electromagnetic pulse, they'd fry any unshielded electronics and the plane would go down with all of them still on it?

He exchanged a panicked look with Maverick, whose stricken expression suggested he'd arrived at the same concern.

Should we stop them? Bruno wondered, and saw the same process reflected across the alpha's face. Brow drawn low in consternation, lips pressed together so tightly that they turned pale, a wild uncertainty cycling through eyes accustomed to certitude.

But this was Naya. Was she worth risking them all?

Bruno's chest tightened even further. He knew his answer. She was worth risking it all.

But would the alpha with the responsibility for an entire pack arrive at the same conclusion?

Maverick pinched the bridge of his nose, but finally nodded a curt affirmative across to Bruno.

He breathed again and hoped with everything he had that they were doing the right thing by placing their trust in these two half-dead mages.

With an audible *crack*, lightning arced through the air in visible streaks of bluish white so bright that the lines of energy left afterimages cycling through Bruno's vision.

Mordecai and Albacus chanted more loudly. The air sparked and hissed and sizzled.

Behind him, several of the pack wolves gasped, but Bruno didn't dare turn. Not for a second would he look away from where Naya lay. Not even to follow the path of the lightning.

The lights flickered in the cabin.

Maverick took a step forward as if to interfere.

"Wait," Bruno whispered, hoping not to interrupt the wizards, praying they wouldn't end up in a nosedive before any of it would matter.

The lights flickered again. Lightning arced some more through the cabin, crashing here and there with miniature booms of thunder, each one causing Bruno's heart to skip a beat, to hold his breath until he confirmed the plane continued to maintain its altitude.

The brothers' voices rose to a crescendo as they grew more persistent in calling out their spell. Jagged streaks of light shot out from both of their palms.

An errant lightning bolt snapped against a window like a whip. A crack spread along the inner pane of plexiglass like a spider's web.

Maverick took another step toward the wizards.

Bruno could feel the mounting panic of the wolves beyond him, but he again refused to look at them, doing all he could to maintain calm and see this through.

"Come on," he rumbled under his breath. "*Mierda*, come on."

The brothers placed their sparking hands atop Naya's wolf body.

She jolted. Her body jerked and jumped.

Over and over.

But her eyes didn't open. Her heart didn't beat. And she didn't draw a single life-sustaining breath.

The wizards withdrew their touch. Their mouths drew still. The spell was over. Complete.

A deafening, heavy, defeated silence swept across the cabin. The occasional crackling of still-dispersing energy cut loudly through the stunned quiet that followed the localized storm.

Mordecai and Albacus looked up, their faces a matching set of defeat. Their arms fell to their sides, faces drawn and tired. There seemed nothing left to say.

Naya lay as wholly still as when Bruno had first

found her, as broken as ever despite the many sutures across her frame.

"No," Bruno said. "No, no, no, *no*. It has to work. Dammit. Motherfucker. *La puta mierda.*"

He ran his touch along Naya's head, down her back, feeling the way her body was crushed in so many places.

Maverick placed a hand on one of Bruno's shoulders.

Bruno shook him off.

Maverick pressed both hands to his shoulders this time, squeezing hard, attempting to pull him away.

But Bruno snarled, whipping around to snap at him, as if Brother Wolf were already free of the cage Bruno kept him in.

Maverick stepped back, but a warning scrawled across his face. The firm set of his eyes and mouth said, *I'm giving you a minute to lose your shit and then I'm intervening again. And next time, I won't let you push me away.*

The alpha was giving him this allowance because he thought Naya was gone. That there was no bringing her back now.

That she was ... dead.

Bruno struggled to complete the thought, the fear that ached like a gaping pit in the center of his being.

A chasm was breaking open inside him. If he let it, he'd never find the way to close it back up. He just knew it.

He pressed his hands to Naya's chest, where he should have felt her lungs inflating and deflating, pushing her chest up and down, her heart pumping blood through her body steadily and pleasantly.

The silence, the stillness, felt more hollow than his insides.

He needed to get in there. To do something. Anything. To keep trying until something finally worked.

"Cut her open," he said aloud before he realized that's what he would say. But once he did, he knew it's what he truly wanted.

Glancing up, he found Scooby. "Open her back up."

"Bruno," Maverick scolded, alpha power pulsing through his words.

Bruno threw that power right back at him, feeling it hit its mark. "No. We can pump her heart manually."

A pause while everyone, including the crazy wizards, studied him.

"I'm no doctor, but I've seen it done in movies. You manually stimulate the heart into pumping. It can be done, right?"

As one, they all looked at Scooby.

"I mean, yeah, theoretically it can work, but—"

"That's all I need," Bruno cut in. He stared at Maverick. "Don't give up on her now."

"I'll never give up on her. She's like a daughter to me."

"What have we got to lose? We've already"— Bruno had to pause to swallow down the lump obstructing his throat. "We've already lost her if we don't do something else. The spell didn't work. Maybe this will."

Maverick deliberated while studying Naya. His eyes welled with what Bruno could only describe as paternal love.

Bruno wasn't the only one breaking here...

"Mav. We gotta try, man. We gotta give it our all. Just like she did."

"She did do the impossible by trying to make it down that rock face," Cleo said. "She fought to survive."

"And we'll keep fighting for her." Maverick nodded. "Open her up, Scooby."

Scooby raced across the cabin, gathering supplies, Cleo trailing him, helping him with what she could.

In minutes he reappeared, hands sterilized and up in front of his face.

"I'll be pumping her heart," Bruno said. He wasn't asking for fucking permission. This was his mate. His woman. His wolf's perfect match.

No one was touching her heart but him.

Scooby looked to Maverick for approval, then nudged Cleo to help Bruno disinfect his hands, a task Bruno found ironic since Naya's wolf could definitely survive germs.

But he didn't complain and soon stood beside his mate, waiting, unable to look away as Scooby cut through his stitches and enlarged the existing incision so Bruno could easily reach into her chest cavity.

This was most definitely not the way he'd imagined he'd first enter her body.

He slid his dominant hand through gaping fur and flesh and blood to find her heart.

Her heart.

The life-giving organ.

"Come on, *mi amor*," he whispered to her, when he'd never called another woman *my love* in his life.

She was the one. The only one.

All that mattered.

After a thick gulp, he wrapped his fingers around her heart, allowed the weight of it to rest in the cup of his palm, and pumped.

Once, twice, thrice.

He paused, waiting.

"Anything?" Maverick asked urgently, though he'd be able to hear as easily as Bruno that her heart hadn't beat.

Yet.

Again. He pumped one, two, three times. Paused, then pumped again, and this time he kept on going. A few dozen times.

He stopped.

He waited.

He listened.

With every fiber of his being, he urged Naya's heart to pump on its own.

To beat. To give life to someone so incredibly special.

He went to pump her heart again, unwilling to give up until he was forced to—

And then...

He stilled completely. Went rigid. Didn't breathe. Didn't think. Didn't inch his fingers around her heart while he waited.

He felt it a moment before it arrived. As a mate would.

Thump.

CHAPTER ELEVEN

NAYA

SEVERAL THINGS HAPPENED AT ONCE. Naya's eyes shot open; her heart thumped erratically, as if it were a wobbly top, causing her stomach to turn, and she sucked in a breath deeper than seemed possible, causing her to cough violently.

The sudden movement made *everything* ache. Not just ache, *hurt*—and badly. Especially her chest.

For a few moments, all she could do was attempt to settle her coughing while moving as little as possible. Every whip of her head as she wheezed hurt too much. Too painful.

A series of alarmed cries reached her from all sides. And a man leaned over her. That much she could tell.

Her eyeballs and throat stung as she coughed and sucked in slivers of breath ... and finally managed to pull in a normal, complete inhale. Her eyes watered while she focused on breathing and studying the man's arms that reached toward her.

His sleeves were pushed up past his elbows to reveal dark lines accentuating the corded muscles of his forearms. The fierce head of a wolf peeked out from beneath his shirt.

Her thoughts foggy, mesmerized by the dark lines inked onto tanned skin, she moved her head slightly, wanting to see where they ended. The motion sent a fresh wave of agony washing through her body.

Fearing she might vomit, she sucked in a sharp breath, unable to temper her reaction to the pain.

Holy hell, how could so many things hurt at once? Shouldn't there be some kind of limit?

Then ... then she realized those masculine arms led *inside* her. That they actually disappeared *into her fucking chest.*

Her *furry* chest.

That's right ... the shift had overtaken her.

She'd been climbing down the mountain. She hadn't made it to the base yet. She hadn't even been able to see bottom through the mist and descending darkness when her wolf ripped through her flesh.

At the memories, Naya attempted to scramble backward, away from the arms that reached into her

—only to feel strong hands at her back, keeping her in place.

Voices were yelling at her, but her pulse whooshed through her mind too loudly to register any words.

Her chest was cut wide open.

Experiencing a panic reminiscent of what she'd felt the moment before she realized she was about to fall—to her death, she'd thought—she followed the hard planes of those strong arms upward. Across a muscled chest.

Up to the beautiful face of the beta wolf of the Andes Mountain Pack.

Bruno.

What was he doing here? With his hands reaching *inside* her?

She glanced up into his face, and his eyes locked on to hers and wouldn't let go.

His mouth was moving. Those beautiful lips were forming words, but *whoosh, whoosh, whoosh* was all that came through.

His brow and forehead were scrunched into hard lines of concern. His eyes were flashing the forest green of his pack's magic, hypnotically keeping her lost in him.

Bruno began a series of theatrically exaggerated in and out breaths. Deep, calming.

He was trying to get her to do the same, so she did, while the memories of her fall crashed together with the current pain, until she feared that if Bruno weren't guiding her back to herself she might pass out again.

Finally, the voices began crystallizing into something intelligible, and she recognized the energy signature of her alpha behind her. It was his hands that pressed against her back, holding her in place.

She trusted Mav implicitly. If he was there, she was safe.

The green flashed in Bruno's eyes a final time before settling enough for her to see the kaleidoscope of blues, browns, and greens behind it.

"Stay with me, *Peligrosa*," he said, his voice as deep as her relief to find herself here with him, with Mav. Safe. Away from the psycho immortal intent on wreaking devastation everywhere she went.

I'm not going anywhere, Naya said, only to later realize she hadn't managed to get the words out. Right. She was a wolf.

Regardless, Bruno's forehead smoothed out as if he'd heard her.

"Don't move, Ni."

That was Maverick, a rough rasp that revealed the emotion he usually hid from her.

Then Cleo's face was pressed next to hers.

"Don't move, girl. Not an inch. We don't want Bruno to cause more damage as he extracts his hands from your heart."

Cleo must have noticed the thousand questions writing themselves across her face, because she added, "He manually pumped your heart. You've been dead for ... well, for too long. Long enough that we started to think we'd lost you for real."

Naya licked her nose, wishing she could speak. That she could tell her and Bruno and Mav how glad she was to be with them. How very glad she was not to be dead.

Cleo's hair, currently black streaked with violet, slid across her face as she pressed a hand gingerly to Naya's neck.

"You punctured an artery in your neck, dislocated both hind legs, broke a few ribs, and nearly snapped in half. You're beat to shit and back. Do *not* move while Bruno pulls out of you."

Cleo smirked at her unintended pun, and Naya wholeheartedly wished she were up to sharing in a chuckle about how Bruno was inside her, just not the way she had imagined. But all Naya could do was blink her eyes in an affirmative way and hold still.

A feat that proved more difficult than she expected when she felt Bruno's forearms and then hands slide out of her rib cage. Pulling through flesh never meant to be stimulated by outside forces.

So this is what it feels like to be disemboweled. Medieval torturers knew what they were doing. It was awful.

When Scooby's face replaced Cleo's to tell her he was going to give her an anesthetic before he sewed her up again, Naya was certain her eagerness at some pain relief showed on her face. In anticipation of it, she closed her eyes, holding the vision of Bruno there behind them.

After seeing him in her dreams, here he was. He'd found her again.

CHAPTER TWELVE

MEILING

BY THE TIME the plane finally touched down, all of Meiling's intentions to map out a master plan had faded into oblivion. Even Sister Wolf was dormant within her, no longer interested in being present for the unrelenting pain the silver caused. Sometime along the endless flight, Meiling had allowed her mind to shut down, to travel to another place where she could pretend she wasn't at the whim of a cruel eternal being. Her fate had shifted from being the pawn of one undying race to that of another.

When vampires lifted her body and carried her from the jet, it was as if she were staring at them through a dense fog. Their faces were nebulous, their scents imprecise, and the air surrounding her muggy but otherwise unremarkable. She missed all the clues of her location. They'd flown long enough that they could be anywhere in the world now.

Either way, the *where* didn't much matter so long as Meiling continued under Cassia's command. Meiling wasn't even in control of her own bodily functions. She couldn't complete the transformation to her wolf without the removal of the silver poison.

At some point, the vampires flung her unceremoniously onto another hard surface, as cold as the floor of the airplane. And finally, when her sanity was on the verge of collapse, they unclasped the silver that bound her. The chink of metal on metal rang through her mind like the chime of an angelic bell, soft and beckoning. Hopeful. She sucked in a shaky inhale while relief began to pour through her like warm liquid in her veins.

A door slammed, a lock tumbled, and silence engulfed her thumping body like a smothering blanket. But the silver was off. She'd recover. She'd renew. Her strength would return, as would her will to rip Cassia's damn throat out in a bloody, glorious mess. All she had to do was give her body time.

She had three days to be in her wolf form. Three nights to complete her shift and allow herself the full power of her healing. Three days before Meiling, the woman who'd devoted her entire life to the study of Seimei Do, re-emerged. Three days to figure how to finish a botched shift, how to kill the unkillable, and to make her way to Naya.

She closed her eyes and willed herself to sleep. She'd suppress every other need but that which fueled her ability to secure her escape and end Cassia.

If Seimei Do had taught her anything, it was that with will, strength, and determination, there was always a way. Success might not arrive in an instant; it might take days, months, or even years.

But Meiling would never stop trying to rid the world of Cassia.

Not until she succeeded—or the immortal did.

Either way, they wouldn't share this world for long.

CHAPTER THIRTEEN

BRUNO

HE DIDN'T WANT to leave Naya, not even to step away for a moment. But it had to be done.

Scooby had sutured Naya back up, and whatever he'd given her was potent enough to knock out a panicked werewolf. Right then, Bruno was grateful Scooby traveled with tranquilizers dosed for an entire herd of elephants. Naya's shifter body would process the medicine too quickly, but at least, until then, she was resting comfortably, which meant she was finally healing.

She was alive.

His mate was here. Breathing, beating, being. She'd stared back into his eyes with an intensity that had Brother Wolf skipping around inside him. Never before had Bruno experienced Brother Wolf so joyous.

Bruno and Naya now had a chance at a life together. Of course, there was the point of having to convince her that he was her mate, that she should spent the rest of her life at his side...

But one thing at a time.

"We need to talk," Bruno told Maverick under his breath before leading the alpha to the back of the plane, next to the restroom, where the engines seemed loudest.

Maverick made sure none of his wolves were close enough to eavesdrop before whispering. "I know what you want to talk about."

Bruno arched a brow and waited.

"Back there, I came to while being carried by my wolves."

So he did know what Bruno wanted to speak with him about. Did he also understand what that must mean?

"I have no memory of what happened immediately before then," Maverick continued. "But I'm guessing I either blacked out from some injury I show no sign of now or..." He trailed off, clearly uncomfortable with the idea.

"You didn't black out," Bruno said. "You went blank. Your eyes, your face. You didn't register when we spoke to you, when we shook you, trying to bring you back."

"Like something took over my consciousness?" The question was so soft, as if once the alpha put it out there he wouldn't be able to tuck the fear back away.

"Yes. Exactly like that," Bruno said. Maverick was alpha to a large pack of wolf shifters. They relied on him for their safety. Dancing around the problem wouldn't do anyone any favors.

Maverick nodded, his mouth pinching with his distress. "You think this *fucking immortal* is using me? Somehow invading my mind and taking over?"

"As crazy as it seems, yes, I think it's likely that you are the spy within your pack."

Maverick chuckled darkly, like the ominous clouds rolling in before a turbulent thunderstorm. "That fucking bitch." He breathed heavily, his nostrils flaring, shaking his head over and again at unaccustomed impotence. "How? How is she doing it? How can we be sure? And how fucking dare she do that to me?"

"We can't be sure it's her, but who else would it be?"

Maverick scowled. "Right. Who else has the kind of power she does? And who else has no problem submitting others to her will, entirely lacking a moral compass?"

"Do you have any sense of what happened while

she ... took over? Is there any remnant of her left behind so we can be sure that's what happened?"

"No. None. If I didn't wake up all of a sudden, buck naked sitting in a chair hold while my wolves ran through the forest, I think I might have no idea anything had happened at all."

"That's terrifying."

"Tell me about it." Maverick blew out a frustrated breath, causing the hair that had tumbled across his forehead to billow. "Tell me more about what it was like on your end."

"One minute you were normal, the next it was like you'd completely checked out. No one was home."

Maverick growled.

"I was running ahead of you, so I didn't see when you came back. But you already know that."

Maverick placed his forehead in his hand for a few moments: "Okay, so what do we know for sure? I met this Cassia before, when she brought Naya to me as a baby. She has crazy magic that has Mordecai and Albacus drooling. They don't seem to know what all she's capable of doing. She's vicious and cruel, and doesn't give a shit how her actions affect others."

"What we don't know, however," Bruno cut in, "is that she's behind your blank-out for sure." When Maverick frowned, Bruno added, "Though it does seem likely. Unless you can think of someone else who might be behind it? We shifters have our fair share of enemies. Nothing like being despised for how we're born..."

"For real." Maverick's gaze sharpened. "No, there's no one else. It's gotta be her. If she managed to get inside my head somehow, which she probably did, then I'm compromised. It's possible that she knows everything that I know. I'm the motherfucking spy in my own pack. I've sworn to defend every single one of my wolves with my dying breath, and here I am, potentially endangering them without even realizing it. That's just wrong, man. So, *so* fucking wrong. I'm gonna choke the life right out of that immortal bitch."

Bruno didn't bother pointing out the definition of the word *immortal*. He was wrestling with the same impulse. The sooner they figured out how to kill Cassia, the better.

And they would find a way. Because they had to.

Cassia had fixated on Naya and Meiling, on the sisters. There could only be one reason for that interest, and that was their connection to the ancestral bloodline of Callan "the Oak" MacLeod. Cassia must want to wipe out all werewolves and spare the hunters the trouble. Why she hadn't killed Naya or Meiling when she first had the chance, Bruno didn't understand—perhaps she wanted them to suffer more before she ended them. She seemed fully capable of that or some equally twisted thinking.

If Cassia had located Naya and Meiling, if she'd *delivered* Naya to her pack, then chances were high that the immortal knew where Lara was as well.

Until they discovered the way to eliminate the immortal, the three sisters would remain in grave danger.

Maverick said, "We need to get back to Colorado, make sure Naya's safe, and then figure out how to get Meiling and kill Cassia."

"But you can't be involved in any of the planning," Bruno said.

"No, no I can't. Which is about as messed up as it gets. I'm the strongest wolf in the pack, and she's effectively benching me. Until we know how she's messing with me, I can't know anything she shouldn't know.

"When we get back, River will have to handle the attack and rescue. He's smart and a good leader. He'll do fine. Until then, you're in charge. I feel your wolf. I know what you're capable of."

"And what will you do?"

"I'm gonna lock myself in the sleeping quarters and do my best not to overhear anything. Whatever information Naya has, I shouldn't hear it. The less I know, the better."

He snarled loudly. "Man, this is so messed up!" His eyes flashed the gold of his pack's magic. Again, he dropped his head into his hands for a few moments, before staring Bruno down.

"I'm entrusting you with the wellbeing of my pack until we get home."

"Then we've come a long way," Bruno said, trying to make light of the situation and failing.

"Don't you dare let me down."

"I would never. I'll treat your pack wolves as if they were my own, I promise you. They're in good hands with me."

Maverick stared into Bruno's eyes so hard that he felt his magic flash. Finally, Maverick nodded curtly. "I'll tell them all. Through the link. And I'm off to take a fucking nap. Like I've got nothing more important to do."

He spun, leaned his hands on a handle bolted into the wall meant for steadying passengers, yanked the bar free of its fastenings, bent the handle in half before tossing it onto the floor, and marched off, his shoulders tighter and stronger than that bar of chintzy metal had been. Moments later, the door to the single private cabin on the plane latched shut with a loud click.

If Cassia had managed to deceive a man as astute and powerful as Maverick, she was even more dangerous than Bruno had realized.

Without hesitation, he started back toward Naya. He could speak to the wizards while he sat by her side. Never had he been more grateful that the peculiar wizards were their allies.

They'd need every single advantage they could get to take Cassia down.

Just as soon as Naya was tucked away somewhere safe and protected.

She'd always come first.

CHAPTER FOURTEEN

CASSIA

CASSIA CLOSED her eyes and pointed her face toward the sun, enjoying the way its heat warmed her skin. She'd always loved this estate of hers in Southern France. It was smaller than most of her properties, but it was well hidden and easily guarded, and it was where she'd directed her team of scientists to make their home base.

"Mistress," Édouard said from behind her, yanking her out of her thoughts. "They are ready for you."

Cassia didn't restrain the grin that split her face nearly in half, though she didn't share it with anyone, not even her dedicated servant.

It was here that Cassia had built a state-of-the-art facility capable of carrying out every scientific feat she could dream of, making her something no other immortal had the imagination to become, a being with the power of two supernaturals in one body. Here at this quaint estate, she'd see the results of a quarter century of planning.

When she spun away from her view of her rose garden, where most of the buds were in bloom, her pleasure was once more concealed, her emotions carefully guarded.

"Wonderful news, Éd. I'll be there shortly. Leave me now."

Édouard bowed his head and turned, disappearing back into the spacious house, pulling the glass doors firmly closed behind him.

For the first time in years, Cassia purposefully thought of her father. Too often he invaded her dreams, where she was powerless to eject him. But now she conjured him up, picturing the stern slant of his brows and mouth; his angular nose slightly too large for his face, somehow managing to make him look distinguished despite its size; his intelligent, piercing eyes the same color as hers continually broadcasting his disapproval. Her father had had everything: riches, power, influence ... a caring wife and a houseful of lovely, beautiful daughters. Her parents' marriage had been arranged, as was common then, but her mother had come to care for her father, or at least to accept his philandering ways and unwavering discipline.

But no matter what Cassia's sisters did to gain his approval, it was never enough. Her father fixated on her alone, as if she had somehow been different or better than them just for sharing his eye color, when the seven sisters all had the same straight black hair and pale, milky skin.

Born and raised in a turbulent time in medieval *Italia*, the sisters had banded together. When their father's attention had been harsh and unwarranted, they'd comforted each other behind closed doors, where he didn't interfere. They'd been more than sisters, they'd been allies, united against a menacing front. They'd been the best of friends, a team victorious for its unity, if nothing else.

But then, their father, who was never content, though the reason for his unhappiness was passing and changing, discovered magic. Not a magic of his own, but merely its existence. That had been enough to possess the man. The idea of magic consumed his every waking moment for long enough that Cassia and her sisters had leaned into the relief of his inattention toward them. He no longer scolded or reprimanded them for little reason. He ceased deciding their every important action. When Cassia's eldest sister reached marrying age, he didn't even arrange a commitment for her, as was expected for the time.

Cassia and her sisters had dared to hope. Only much later did Cassia discover how very dangerous hope was.

When her father met the dark mage Senarus, he disappeared from their lives entirely. Their mother used the opportunity to make their house a home, managing her husband's land holdings to provide for their family.

Years later, after their hearts had grown light and buoyant, their father returned. His eyes, once violet like hers, were a hardened black. One by one, he took Cassia's sisters away, and none of them ever returned. Only when it was her turn, the last of them, did Cassia understand what was happening.

Senarus had convinced their father that immortality was possible, that he was on the precipice of developing a spell that would harness the power of eternity within a human shell. Six attempts on six beautiful sisters failed. The seventh saw success.

Cassia was forced to watch Senarus cast immortality upon her father amid the corpses of her sisters, discarded on the damp and dirty floor of the mage's dungeon-cum-laboratory as if their lives meant nothing. As if they had no value beyond how they could serve the man who'd seeded them.

When Cassia asked her father to end her life so she could join her sisters in death, he'd only stared at her. She'd never forget the words he said to her after she'd begged, or the cruel bite to them: "You were the only one to matter of them all. And now you'll never die. From my efforts, glory is yours. You'll be at my side forever."

Cassia watched her mother age and weaken and die, and all the while she studied and plotted and planned. It took her centuries, but she finally proved her father wrong. She'd never be at his side again. He'd never be anything again.

So that he could live forever, he'd cursed her to an eternity of solitude. Despite his claims that she was the only one among her sisters to matter, the greater truth was that they'd all been experiments. Only after Senarus' spell had taken with Cassia did her father subject himself to the same.

Beneath the warm sunlight of near summer, Cassia caressed a single rose, its petals a bright salmon pink. Despite the fact that over a thousand years had passed since she'd last seen her sisters' faces, she conjured them up in her mind, nearly able to hear the precise tone of their laughter—but not quite. She couldn't remember what their voices sounded like anymore, or the warmth of their touch. The passing years had robbed her of so much.

"This is for you, *belle*," she whispered, her words as soft and evanescent as her ancient memories. For them, she'd make the most of the eternity she was forced to endure without them. They'd want that for her. If their father was to sentence her to immortality without them, then they'd want her to revel in it just to spite him. They'd want her to achieve what he'd never managed. To be what he'd never even dreamt of being.

Gingerly, Cassia pressed a kiss to a petal, imagining it was one of the smooth cheeks of her sisters. She thought she might feel their spirits with her, and before she could doubt that, to wonder if it was nothing more than her vain imaginings, she spun and marched across the house, out another doorway and through another garden, and finally into the outbuilding her scientists had transformed into a state-of-the-art lab. Magic was more ancient than she was, from a time long before beeping machines. But whatever Cassia had to do to increase her chances at success, she'd do it.

No stone unturned. No chance squandered.

Blinds were drawn, recessed lighting the only steady source of illumination. Shiny equipment of all sorts dotted the many tabletops, and a glass-door refrigerator spanned a dozen feet of wall. Cassia didn't know what exactly most of the machinery did, but it was expensive, the best of the best. The air was crisp and temperature-controlled, smelling slightly of ozone and disinfectant. Her scientists were fastidious, as eager as she was to achieve the breakthrough of the century—of the millennium! A half dozen of them, men and women, stood at attention in bright, white lab coats. Their eyes tracked her every movement, half of them afraid to make eye contact when she glanced their way, and the other half afraid not to. But she passed them without pausing, eager to see the proof of her many efforts. They didn't realize, of course, that they wouldn't be around to enjoy their achievements, not after they completed the work she required of them.

At the very back of the large, open room lay Meiling, strapped down to a medical gurney.

Cassia hadn't bothered with the deceptions she'd employed with Davina. There was no point. Meiling had already figured out that things weren't as they seemed, and that Cassia was the predator here.

When Cassia drew near, her pulse sped up in anticipation. This could be the time. No one said she'd need all her girls—all her tries—to get this right. It could happen this time. Today. Now. Excitement raced across her skin like a sudden sharp frigid wind. She tingled all over.

When she leaned over the girl, Meiling thrashed

against her bindings, laced with silver to counteract her latent werewolf strength, and spewed some biting Chinese at her.

When Cassia didn't react, unsure what the girl had said—though the gist wasn't too difficult to guess at—Meiling spat on her.

Cassia froze while Édouard advanced, a silk handkerchief at the ready, wiping away the spittle with a censuring look at the girl.

But Cassia only smiled. What did she care what the girl did? She could complain and insult her all she wanted. Only one of them there was an immortal. Only one of them would live forever.

Only she could make the most of the wolf shifter magic wasted on the girl. Her scientists had figured out how to break the bond between werewolves and moon cycles. When Cassia became a werewolf, she'd be able to transform at will, just like a true wolf shifter.

There was no more reason to delay. She had all she needed.

"Hello, Meiling," Cassia said in a smooth seductive roll as she stepped to the edge of the medical bed. "I have something for you. I've been waiting a very long time to give it to you."

"Whatever it is, I don't want it," the girl said, a

faint Chinese accent tingeing her rebellion. "You can shove it straight up your ass."

"Oh, Meiling, you naïve girl. I wasn't asking. Don't you know? With magic like mine, you're never given a choice. Neither of us have a choice in what happens next. Our fate was decided a very long time ago."

When Cassia lowered her face to Meiling's, the girl pulled back as far as she could go against the padded medical bed, thrashing side to side.

"Get away from me," she snapped, but even then a noticeable helplessness flashed across her eyes and creased the skin of her forehead. Her lower lip wobbled and the girl bit it to keep from revealing her fear—too late.

"I cannot, Meiling," Cassia said. "Girls like us never get to decide our destinies."

"You're deciding to do whatever it is you're about to do to me. No one's making you."

"I am deciding and I'm also not. I am who I am now, but I didn't choose it. I didn't want it. I would have never agreed to pay the price of my magic. But now that I am an immortal, I must honor that nature. It's the way of things. I must make the best of my fate, as so must you. I'm an immortal, so my needs supersede yours. I alone will live until the end of the world, and perhaps even beyond that.

You will be gone soon. Your very existence is fleeting."

Cassia paused while the faces of her sisters flashed across her mind's eye, the haunting echo of their laughter trailing as they disappeared from the only place they still existed.

Cassia straightened, her gaze unfocused as she stared at a blank wall above Meiling's head. "I didn't used to be this way. I wasn't all that different from you at one time, wanting little more than to be with my sisters. To make the best of my life. I had six sisters. You only have three, but it's the same, I think."

Meiling released her lip. "Three sisters? You're including me in that count?"

"No, but I suppose you're nearly right anyway. One of you is dead. Davina wasn't strong enough. I think you will be, however."

"Davina? This Davina is a sister of mine? You're sure?"

Cassia dragged her attention back to the girl she'd spent so much effort cultivating. "Of course I'm sure. If not for me, not a single one of you would have ever been born."

A few seconds passed, before Meiling eked out, "What?" in a squeak.

Cassia chuckled, but she was too tired for real

mirth. Suddenly the thousand years she'd lived felt like a hundred times that.

"There is no reason not to tell you now. Your destiny? That of you and your sisters? How you are all the blood heirs of the great and mighty Callan 'the Oak' MacLeod? That was one of my most ingenious moments."

"What—what are you saying?" Meiling asked after swallowing hard enough that Cassia heard her throat move.

"That you will not save the werewolves from their natural decline no matter if you reproduce as plentiful as rabbits."

Cassia could practically feel the gears turning in Meiling's mind.

"You ... you made all that up?" Meiling asked. "Is that what you're saying?"

"Yes. It was a stroke of brilliance, wouldn't you say? I needed a story that would ensure all four of you were kept alive and safe until I was ready for you. There's nothing humans like better than a good old-fashioned savior story. Pretty brilliant, eh?"

Meiling was silent, eyes vibrating with the thoughts racing behind them.

"That's all right. You don't have to say it. I know. I picked your parents. They were desperate to breed. It was so easy to tell them what they wanted to hear, to fund their in-vitro treatments. They called me their savior."

Cassia cocked her head to one side, glancing down at the girl. "Ironic, no?"

"Psychotic, more like. You take narcissism to a whole new clinical level. They'd probably dedicate entire textbooks to you if they knew about you."

Cassia smiled. "Thank you."

"It wasn't a compliment."

"It was, you just didn't realize it. I've always been intelligent, but time has allowed me to become extraordinary."

Meiling strained her neck to stare at Cassia head-on. "Did you kill my real parents? Or was that actually hunters?"

"Hunters serve many purposes, but I don't hire them to do my work for me. At least, not the work that is really important. I contain the power of life and death. I'm as close to a god as you'll see wandering this earth. I kill, and I make alive."

"So you convinced our parents to do in vitro, then made us all your guinea pigs, and spread us out away from each other, making us believe we were the saviors of werewolfkind? Did I get that right?"

"Yes, close enough."

"And did you kill this other sister of mine, Davina?"

"Yes, but not on purpose. She simply wasn't strong enough to survive my immortality magic."

"And what are you going to do to me?"

"Infuse you with my immortality magic."

"Like you did her?"

"Yes, but you're much stronger than her. I can tell."

"Based on what, exactly?"

"On your ability to survive the great Grand Master Ji-Hun and all his nonsense. He's developed quite the demanding system up there in his little world of a monastery."

"There is much one could say about the master vampires, and especially about Grand Master Ji-Hun," Meiling said, "and most of it would be true. But the Seimei Do martial art he developed? Brilliant."

Cassia nodded once. "I'm glad you think so. I'm counting on it to give you the strength and courage you'll need to survive an infusion of my magic. It is not made for the weak."

Once more, she couldn't stop her thoughts from whisking across the likenesses of her sisters. They'd been filled with joy and beauty; they'd been the brightest and lightest beings she'd ever known. And that lightness hadn't given them the strength to survive the immortality spell. Only she had the seed of darkness in her necessary for immortality to stick. She'd been the only one to look more like their father than any of the others, to *be* more like their father.

Cassia forced her attention back on the present, where it mattered. She might have started out more like her father than any of her sisters, but she was about to do the one thing that would make her entirely unlike him. And so much more powerful than he'd ever come close to being.

"It's been fun chatting with you, Meiling," Cassia said. "I didn't expect that, I admit. But I'm impatient now. It's time to begin."

Without glancing around her, she called out, "Édouard." The vampire was never far away.

In a second, he was bowing at her side. "Mistress, how may I be of service?"

"Tell them I'm ready."

She didn't wait for the scientist to assemble around her. There was nothing they needed to do at first beyond observe.

Cassia lowered her face once more to Meiling's.

The girl's eyes widened as if she were a rabbit who'd lost the chase to a swooping hawk. Cassia wrapped her hands around Meiling's skull like talons.

"No," Meiling breathed.

"You know what they call me?"

Meiling gulped. "The Kiss of Death."

"Then you know what's coming. In a way, life and death, they are not so very different from what we imagine."

"They seem pretty different to me."

"Not for long."

And then, before Meiling could say anything else, Cassia pressed her lips against hers. For a few moments, she kissed her, though the girl didn't reciprocate.

Then Cassia pried her mouth open and, instead of sucking out her life force as Cassia usually did, she pulsed her immortality magic out through her breath.

When Cassia felt a tug on her own magic reserves, she pulled back. At that point, her magic would regenerate and she would be no different. It was what had happened with Davina. Any more and Cassia would be weakened, unacceptable under any circumstances.

When Meiling coughed and spat, Cassia allowed hope to burgeon throughout every part of her being. Attitude was welcome now. It meant the girl was as strong as Cassia had hoped.

But when the girl began to convulse, her limbs straining against her restraints, Cassia sighed and stepped out of the way.

Her team swarmed in, defibrillator paddles at the ready, adrenaline shots already loaded in syringes.

"Are you all right, Mistress?" Édouard asked, attention only on her, not the seizing girl who'd now begun foaming at the mouth.

"I suppose, Éd. I'm just ready for this to take. It's been too long in the making for this to fail."

"Agreed, *Madame*. I am hopeful this time the experiment will take."

Cassia looked away from Meiling, to the slices of her she could make out from behind the backs of her scientists, bent over the girl, and to Édouard.

His face was open, entirely lacking in guile.

She smiled at him. "You're good to me, Éd."

He smiled back. "I do my best. Shall I draw Mistress a relaxing bath?"

After a final glance at Meiling, who looked to be careening down the same path as Davina had, Cassia nodded. "Yes. And bring me a bottle of Cru Beaujolais."

With that, Cassia crossed the lab and exited into the bright sunshine. Not even that managed to warm her insides.

CHAPTER FIFTEEN

BRUNO

NEVER HAD time slunk along so slowly. Each of the three days until the full moon waned had felt like twenty at least. Bruno understood that the timing of the full moon was partially fortuitous since a werewolf's healing was more accelerated while they were in their wolf forms, but if the full moon hadn't risen when it had, Naya wouldn't be in the awful shape she was. She might have actually made it to the bottom of that insane cliff. He still couldn't believe she'd made as much progress as she had. Her fellow pack wolves hadn't been exaggerating when they said she was one of the foremost rock climbers in the world.

But, like everything else about her, Naya's skill was secret. He wanted to unearth every one of her mysteries. To excavate her world. To join together and make it theirs. In a hurry to learn everything about her, he'd familiarized himself with every one of her silvery spots, the exact shape of her muzzle, and the precise pitch of her growl when she'd come awake after the tranquilizer.

Then, while running his hands along her fur, he'd spent the rest of the flight back to the Rocky Mountain Pack's land in the Moonlit Mountains, Colorado, talking with Albacus and Mordecai, who grew odder and more interesting with every new fact Bruno discovered about them. Even groggy and in great pain, Naya seemed to follow their conversation.

The wizards thought it was very likely that Cassia had found a way to infiltrate Maverick's thoughts, though they weren't certain how exactly she was doing it. Apparently, there were several options. She could be reading his thoughts, an invisible presence filtering through his mind; or she could be influencing his thoughts, injecting her ideas into his consciousness so that he believed them to be his own—she could even be having full-on conversations with him, where Maverick answered her without his knowledge. Every possibility made Bruno's skin crawl.

This immortal was the worst of news from every angle they examined her.

Though Mordecai and Albacus seemed unreasonably excited at the challenge she presented, they hadn't yet arrived on a foolproof way to take her out. Bruno was certain of it; he checked on them nearly as often as he checked on Naya, and he'd barely left her side. But Naya was sleeping again, and Maverick had evicted whatever shifter usually occupied the cabin on the other side of Naya's, giving it to the wizards while they were there. Maverick hadn't said, since he was locked up in his own cabin to the left of Naya's, continuing his self-imposed isolation, but River had suggested the alpha wanted the mages nearby in case Cassia should get past their many defenses and surprise them.

Now that Bruno had passed on the mantle of leadership to River, as Maverick wished, his priority was Naya. He got her food and water; he slept at her side on the bed, atop the duvet.

They hadn't yet bonded as mates—that would require a conversation they could only have after she returned to her human form—but her wolf hadn't pushed him away. Not even when her injured state might have made her wary of a non-pack shifter she hardly knew.

He hoped that meant she already realized they were mates too.

And though the energy of Naya's wolf was far

from settled, she spent most of the time since their arrival at her home sleeping. Maverick had carried her into her cabin before recusing himself, and as if she knew how quickly danger could—and might—arrive, she focused on healing.

Beyond the walls of her small cabin, the Rocky Mountain Pack was keeping as busy as an ant colony, shoring its defenses for wartime, training at all hours, planning and prepping, which wasn't an easy feat when their adversary was powerful beyond measure.

Bedding crinkled behind him, drawing Bruno out of his troubled thoughts. He turned from where he'd stood at the window, peering absently out at the pack wolves coming and going, to discover Naya staring at him, alert behind the eyes of her wolf.

"*Hola, Peligrosa.* So good to see you awake." He walked toward her, sitting atop the bed at her side. She was finally alert, yes, but she still hadn't stood on her own. She lay on her side, relieving the pressure from her still-healing midsection.

Bruno resisted the urge to reach out and touch her. With her attention pinned on him the way it was, he became acutely aware of the fact that he alone had decided she was his mate. What would she think of that? He'd heard stories about mates, of course. It seemed that every shifter who'd been fortunate enough to find their match couldn't help but recount what it felt like, to find that perfect pairing to their entire being. Both human and wolf. Both parties always just ... knew.

Would Naya?

Before he'd found her, he'd already thought himself certain of the role she'd play in his life. But only once he spotted her at the base of Shèng Shān Mountain did he discover just how sure he was.

His entire body zinged at her proximity. His skin tingled all over. Brother Wolf all but pranced like a loon at seeing her there, on the bed, *safe*—for now, at least.

"You scared me," he told her. "I thought I was going to lose you when I'd only just found you."

She didn't react. Simply continued to watch him. Her golden eyes seemed to pierce through skin and pretenses to where they examined his very soul.

Never one to fidget, he shifted on the bed, feeling bare and exposed. He crossed his legs and his arms, then identified them as defensive postures, and forced himself to unwind his limbs.

"We..." he started, then turned to glance out the window, breaking the trance of her unnerving examination. Clearing his throat, he faced her again. "We have a lot to talk about."

Though it wasn't really *a lot*. Just one thing. One point that he wanted to shout from the rooftops.

We are mates, Naya, he wanted to say, shocked to find how much courage the admission required. He was the beta of a strong pack, for fuck's sake. His pack's magic had chosen him because he had the strength to fill the role. And not just fill it, persevere in it. To guide his pack as well as Lara, if necessary.

But the one word—*mate*—stuck on his tongue, suddenly thick and unwieldy.

The man who had the courage to face down any enemy for the sake of his wolves couldn't admit to one plain fact out of fear that it wasn't actual fact, but a deluded hope he'd somehow fabricated out of his desperation to feel that seen, that known.

Brother Wolf whined inside him, unable to understand Bruno's hesitation. Here she was at last. They'd traveled from South America to North, and then to Asia and back, all to find her.

Now she lay within arm's reach ... and Bruno couldn't bring himself to bridge the divide. To admit to his deepest yearnings.

Cobarde, he admonished himself when he'd never had reason to call himself a coward before.

"I..." he began anew, this time determined to lay his heart bare. *He* knew she was his mate. His body, mind, and heart were aligned in this knowing. His *wolf* was even more certain than he was, stuck on the obstacles of the rational mind.

"We..." He inhaled deeply, closing his eyes for a moment. "The moment I first saw you, I knew there was something different about you."

She chuffed.

"Beyond the fact that you are my alpha's twin sister. It wasn't just that which had me captivated." He ran his hands through his hair, flushing at how difficult something so self-evident had become. "*Bueno*, I suppose I didn't realize exactly what had me captivated at first, beyond your obvious beauty, of course."

Again, she chuffed. Had she been in her human shell, she'd have snorted.

"Look, this isn't easy for me. I thought it would be, but now that you're here, like this—could you maybe stop staring at me like that? It makes it hard to think. Not that I need to think about what to say to you, I already know. I mean, I don't know what to say, but I do know what I mean. *Dios mío.*" He slapped his hands against his thighs. "I sound nothing like my usual self. Forgive me." Then he grimaced. What on earth was he asking forgiveness for? She was his *mate*.

Just as he opened his mouth for what he hoped would finally be clear, coherent, and eloquent expression of their fated love, Naya's eyes widened and she yelped in surprise.

"What? What is it?" he asked urgently, running his hands along her body, careful of her injuries, frantic to determine the newest source of her discomfort. To soothe and comfort her.

To be everything to her that a mate was supposed to be.

In response to his question, her wolf body began to creak and groan, elongating and tearing apart before rebuilding anew.

"You're shifting," he whispered, unable to help himself from stating the obvious.

Rarely had he witnessed Lara shifting back after the full moon began to wane. She almost always spent her time as a wolf prowling the forest far beyond their home, leaving Bruno in charge of the pack in her absence.

Now, he couldn't tear his eyes away from her twin, wondering briefly what Lara would think of the existence of a sister. Or of Bruno's desire to claim her as his.

Aware that Naya's shifts were prolonged and painful, he waited. But Naya was a wolf one moment, and less than a minute later she was a woman.

A fully naked woman.

An entirely glorious woman whose body was pure perfection.

As she lay there, panting, shock evident across her face, he couldn't help but study her every peak and valley. The marvelous curve of her hips, waist, and breasts. The way her nipples were pink and pert, small rosebuds waiting to blossom beneath his touch.

His gaze skimmed the pale skin of her throat, the way her pulse throbbed. He could see, hear, and *feel* it as it mirrored the accelerated thumping of his own heart. Her strong shoulders, her defined arms, her hands and slender fingers. The waves of golden hair fanning out behind her.

And then he couldn't help but trail his attention across her injuries. A thick stretch of raw pink skin traced from beneath one plump breast, across her torso, to end at the rise of one hip. The skin had stitched together, but it would still take time before she was ready to resume ordinary activities. Her neck sported a round, puckered scar that was already so small that he figured it might disappear entirely once her healing was complete. Her many scrapes and cuts were already gone without a trace.

Her time as a wolf had served her well. She'd healed quickly. But her injuries had been grave. They'd almost stolen her from him.

"Wow," Naya said on a rushed exhale long before

he was finished examining her. To be fair, he probably could have gawked at her for the rest of the day and into the night and still not had his fill.

"That went fast. And it was all but painless." She grinned. "It was almost worth dying to finally get a fucking easy shift for once."

She rolled onto her back, looking up at the wooden beams of the ceiling. "I could get used to this."

For as nervous as he'd been just moments before, she was notably calm. Considering all that had happened to her since he'd last seen her in her human form, she was remarkably nonchalant.

She sighed happily a few times, then turned her head toward him. "Shit's gotten real, and I doubt we'll have a lot of time to ourselves, especially not once Mav realizes I'm back to myself. So why don't we deal with that while we still can?"

Her smile turned wicked and she winked at him.

He flushed like a timid bride, wondering what the hell was wrong with him.

There could be no doubting what the *that* she referred to was.

Naya had pushed up onto her elbow and was staring straight at the blatantly hard erection he'd done his best to ignore, not wanting to appear as if his body's needs were more important than his heart's.

This was his mate.

He wanted to do right by her from the start.

"Oh man," she said. "I can see you're all up in your head. That's no good. That's where things get all messy and complicated. So before you start stammering again, let me cut to the chase. We're mates."

Brother Wolf threw his head back and howled, filling Bruno's body up inside with a raucous and loud certainty.

The human side of him went tight all over in anticipation, in disbelief that he'd actually just heard those words slip past this beautiful woman's lips.

"That's what you were trying to get at earlier, right?"

He nodded.

"Well, I figured it out too. Nothing like nearly dying to put things into perspective and crystallize some truths for you."

"You didn't nearly die. I think you might have actually died."

"Yeah, me too." This time, her voice was soft, weighed down by the magnitude of all they'd endured since meeting.

But then she cleared the melancholy with a quick shake of her head. "All the more reason to *carpe diem* the hell out of life, am I right? We have a lot to talk about and a lot to deal with."

She smiled at him, this time more demurely, revealing to him that this connection they were beginning to explore between them was as magical and important to her as it was to him. "I don't want to think about the real world yet. I just want to be grateful I'm here, alive, mending back into one piece. That I managed to escape when it didn't seem at all possible. That I'm here." She glanced up at him from beneath long lashes. "That I'm here with *you*."

She fiddled with a loose thread on the comforter. "You know, when you grow up like I did, always knowing the needs of future werewolfkind come before your own ... well, I never let myself consider too much whether or not I'd have a mate, and if I did, if I'd have the chance to find him before I was forced to have kids and pass on the genes that make me resilient enough to carry the werewolf banner. There was always the chance I'd have to just come together with the strongest male werewolf I could find to fulfill my duty. And then if my mate came along later, well, then I'd be shit out of luck. I'd already had someone else's baby. So I didn't let myself dwell on it too long..."

Once more, she looked up at him, this time holding his gaze, a vulnerability that felt much like his evident in her eyes. "I dreamt of you. While I was gone. When Cassia had me, I dreamt of you. That's how I first figured out we were mates. And now ... now that I've spent the last few days with you, my wolf is sure. I'm ... I'm sure."

He nodded, willing himself to believe that this wasn't just another dream, that this was actually happening. He was this lucky. "I dreamt of you too. I figured out that you are my mate the first time you were taken. I, um, well, I actually slept in your room because I needed to feel connected to you."

He'd save the admission of how he'd pleasured himself in her shower, consumed with images of her and her body, for another time, once they knew each other better. When he was ready to share every bit of himself with her, there'd be no secrets between them.

"Maverick let you sleep here? Really?"

"He wasn't happy about it, but yes."

"Wow, the old man's come a long way."

"I don't think he's had much of a choice."

"No, I guess not."

They were both silent for a few moments, reflecting on what had gone down over the last week.

"See?" she said, interrupting the rapidly descending heaviness. "Thinking is no good. I'm tired of thinking. There are too many problems and none with easy solutions." A pause. "We're going to have to deal with Cassia, and trust me when I say there's no guarantee we'll survive her. I want to forget for just a little while. I want to celebrate that I've found my mate in a life when it wasn't at all guaranteed."

She stared straight into his eyes, her own blazing the bright gold of her pack's magic. "I want to know what it feels like to bond with my mate. What it's like to actually have one." Only the briefest of hesitations. "Will you join with me? Will you mate with me?" She laughed nervously. "Before life gets really cray-cray."

But Bruno was incapable of joking now, or even of laughing. His entire body was on fire, his being alight with the enticing thought of connecting with the only woman in this entire world fashioned precisely for him.

He inched toward her on the bed. "There's nothing, and I do mean *nothing*, I want more."

The mirth had dropped from her face and voice. "Then let's get you out of these clothes. You have far too many on."

He all but jumped up to obey, but then...

"What about your injuries? You seriously almost died just a few days ago. You're still—"

"In delicate condition, yes, I realize. But the tightness of my scars only serves to remind me how lucky I am to have this chance. Right now. With you. Besides, I know you'll be careful with me."

"So careful," he whispered. "You're a treasure."

"Then let's start with those jeans of yours. I want to see what's straining to get out like that."

This time, he couldn't help but chuckle. She was fiery, no doubt.

He stood to comply.

CHAPTER SIXTEEN

NAYA

HER BODY ACHED ALL OVER, not just where she'd busted open, nearly breaking in half. The jarring impact of the fall she'd taken from such a great height throbbed throughout her entire body, a dull but constant reminder of how close she'd come to losing everything. She had no doubt she'd looked awful when they'd first found her at the base of Shèng Shān Mountain. If she still felt this sore after three days of dedicated healing in her wolf form, she understood precisely why Bruno had rarely left her side, and why Maverick had done the opposite, barely seeing her at all, when she was certain the protective father figure in him wanted to check on her constantly to verify she was okay.

Though Naya had been in her wolf form, she'd heard everything Bruno and the strange wizards had said—while she was awake anyhow. Naya had already realized that Cassia was a terrible threat, unpredictable in her abilities, wholly lacking in mercy and compassion, vicious and calculating. But to know she'd been able to convert Mav into a spy of his own pack? Of *her*, when he took his oath to protect her so seriously? Cassia was a threat perhaps none of them, not even the translucent mage brothers, were equipped to deal with. And that was before Naya even started thinking about Cyrus, the other immortal who had powers they were unprepared to combat.

So she followed her own advice and forced away her worries, the concerns that nagged at her with unrelenting persistence, and directed her attention only to the man in front of her stepping out of his pants.

Her mate.

The thought was exhilarating and slightly terrifying, as if it were too good to be true, and he might suddenly vanish.

When his jeans hit the floor next to his boots, he peeled off his t-shirt, also tossing it aside. He remained in nothing more than boxer briefs that left little to the imagination, but just enough to have her squirming at the sight of how hard he was for her. His erection strained against the fabric of his shorts, and she'd bet on the snake eventually winning that battle.

His body was taut with muscles, his abdomen flat and tight beneath a dusting of dark hair. He was as fit as any of her fellow Rocky Mountain Pack adventurers.

And finally—*finally!*—she got to check out the extent of that glorious ink as it wrapped around his torso and arms. Lines wove to trace out tribal symbols that meant nothing to her but she imagined meant something to him, encasing the head of a fierce wolf.

She ran her teeth across her bottom lip before noticing what she'd done. She would've laughed at herself and her stereotypical behavior, but she couldn't stop ogling long enough to properly reflect.

She hadn't gotten to choose her mate; fate, or her wolf, or perhaps even some other invisible force, had chosen him for her. But had she gotten to choose, she couldn't have picked a finer male specimen. If this was whom she was meant to reproduce with and extend the werewolf bloodline, creating babies able to withstand the intensity of werewolf magic, then bring it on.

When she finally noticed that he was just standing there, at the edge of the bed, doing nothing, she reluctantly dragged her gaze up to his face.

"What is it? Why'd you stop? What's wrong?"

There was entirely too much fabric between her and what she was sure was going to be the best time of her life thus far.

He cleared his throat awkwardly, then sat on the bed next to her, trailing hungry eyes across the length of her body before pinning them on her own.

"Are you sure you want to do this now? Would it not be better to wait until you heal? You do look quite hurt still..."

"Of course it would be better to wait." She pushed up onto both elbows and the scar across her torso pulled at her skin; she grimaced before she could stop herself.

"See. We should wait," he said. "We have the rest of our lives together to make love."

The rest of our lives. His words echoed through her head. That was obviously what they were talking about as mates, but her mind still struggled to register that this was finally happening to her. She'd been doomed from the start, her parents killed before she'd even had the chance to know them. Good things hadn't happened easily for her.

But this time, something amazing was happening. To her. Something incredible.

She smiled despite the tenderness that stretched across the many sites of injury.

"*Peligrosa*, we don't need to rush. I want to take

my time getting to know your body. *Loving* your body. Showing you exactly how magnificent I think it is..."

He traced the tips of his fingers down one arm, back up again, then to swirl around one breast— mindful of her scar.

She shivered as a massive tingle raced down her body, all the way to her toes. "Well, you'd better not be doing that if you're trying to convince me to hold up."

"I'm not trying to convince you of anything. I'm not in the mood to wait myself."

"Clearly." She pointed a look at his groin.

"But you aren't just any woman. You're my mate. Of everyone in this world, you are the one who most deserves me taking the time to do things the right way the first time."

Naya angled her body away from him in a way she thought imperceptible, but wasn't. He arched a brow at her in question.

"Newsflash, buddy. No woman wants to hear about other women, even if you're telling her she's special among your many conquests."

"My many conquests?" he echoed, the second brow rising to meet the first. "I think perhaps my English isn't as strong as I thought. I'm not following."

"Never mind." She purposefully kept her eyes trained on his face, refusing to be tempted just then by all his body had to offer. "Maybe you're right. Let's just wait." Then she frowned, becoming fully aware she was just being petulant. She didn't want to wait. Oh no, she didn't want to wait another second, injuries and crazy immortals be damned.

He was a sexy-ass wolf shifter who looked to be in his mid- to late-twenties. *Of course* he'd had sex before her. Wolf shifters were notorious for their sexual appetites—men and women. She was the rare exception, the werewolf so "special" and protected that no one dared touch her, lest they incur the wrath of the mighty Maverick Dune.

"What happened?" Bruno asked. "I thought you didn't want to wait when we're in as much danger as we are?"

She scowled. "*We* aren't in danger, just I am. I'm Cassia's target. You could just walk away and never look back."

His brows pinched together to form a groove of confusion. "Why would I walk away? You're my mate." He frowned. "Am I not expressing myself correctly in my English? I don't understand what's happening."

Neither did Naya. Not exactly. She could tell she was reading between the lines of what he was saying and reacting to those inferences, but she couldn't seem to stop herself from doing so. Why would he stick around? He was the beta of another pack halfway across the world from there. And he could lead a life more or less free of all these troubles. Only the usual hunters would be after him for being a shifter, not the big bads that were after her. His life could still be normal ... if he just walked away from this.

Her body scooted away on the bed before her mind caught up with the why of the movement.

He reached for her, his gentle touch turning her face toward his. "*Peligrosa*, what's happening right now? I don't want to hurt you by making love to you when you've already been through so much, but I don't want to let you go for the wrong reasons."

He waited for her to say something. She didn't.

"If you want to wait to do this right, then I understand. But if you want to *carpe diem* life, as you said, then don't walk away." Again, he waited. "At least not without telling me why. I need to understand."

At the sincerity welling in his eyes, she wanted to tell him, she really did. But she hadn't figured it out yet herself. If she felt this raw and vulnerable *before* they made love, what would she feel like during? The thought made her want to scamper farther away from him. She made herself stay.

When he continued to wait without pressuring or otherwise hurrying her, despite the erection that continued to bulge obviously in his boxers, her shoulders relaxed, her body softened, and she wanted to give him something, even if it wasn't the full truth.

"I've never been with a man before." She heard the words come out of her mouth before she'd composed them properly. She hurried to amend, "I mean, well, what I mean is that I've never had sex before. With a man. With anyone."

The words were streaming out of her mouth without forethought. And she'd never been one to fluster overly much ... but Bruno was so compassionate and so beautiful and so much ... her mate. Sister Wolf sang a continuous tune inside her, confirming the veracity of this claim.

Bruno wasn't going anywhere. Her rational mind registered this fact just fine. Mates were for life. Once they found each other, they never wanted to be apart. It would be no different for them.

Was it because her parents had been murdered? Or was it because of how easily she'd been snatched, by Meiling, then Cyrus, and then Cassia? Was she having abandonment issues? Or fear of stability issues?

She snarled at herself, sick of the psychoanalysis already.

Only then did she notice that Bruno continued to wait for her, his eyes soft, a small smile turning up his beautiful mouth.

"Naya, *amor mío.*"

Naya's entire body tensed without seeming reason. *Amor mío.* Those words she understood: *my love.* How long had she dreamt that the curse of her destiny might allow her to find someone to share her life with that would see her this way? Speak to her like this? Longer than she'd allowed herself to admit, even to herself. Not even to Clove. It was a dangerous dream to have, too hopeful when her life wasn't her own. When so many werewolves depended on her.

Bruno slid toward her, his fingers caressing loose strands of her hair as they cascaded over one bare shoulder.

"I am glad you've never made love with anyone before," he said, and Naya realized with a start that she'd moved on to an entirely different conversation in her head. "It's what I would have hoped for, had I allowed myself to hope that I'd find you."

She peeked up at him from beneath her hair. Could it really be that he'd had thoughts so much like her own?

"I've waited for you too," he added.

"Wait, what?"

"Of course I've waited for you."

"But ... really?"

"Yes, *mi amor*. When I had a chance at making love for the first time with my mate, why would I ever disparage that opportunity for something so sacred?"

Naya blinked. Bruno was sounding more and more like a dream man by the second. Maybe she *was* dreaming. She squinted at him, trying to discern if there were any signs that this was indeed a dream. Maybe she was still in Cassia's clutches and the asshole woman had her under her thrall, causing delusional fantasies...

His warm, strong hand settled at her shoulder. "*Peligrosa*, are you all right? Am I upsetting you?"

Naya forcefully shook her head, mostly to knock free the annoying thoughts that kept getting in her way. "I just can't believe you've been waiting." She gulped, unsure if she could get the next words out. "For me."

His smile was melty warm. "Why wouldn't I? The bond between true mates is supposed to be magical."

"It is." She drew the words out.

"My pack is small, smaller than yours."

"Oh, so you just didn't have many women to choose from?"

"No, I had sufficient women to choose from. But

none of them are my mate. I knew early on that none of them were meant for me." He shrugged. "So I just hoped you were out there somewhere and I waited."

"And you waited," she repeated, still struggling to accept that things could be this easy.

He nodded. "Isn't that why you waited too?"

"More or less." There'd be time later to admit that was only half of the reason why she'd waited. Or perhaps it was the whole reason, and she'd just been kidding herself thinking she hadn't connected with someone because *they* didn't want to. There were plenty of men in her pack who were attracted to her; they'd never concealed that from her, even with Maverick hovering around her like an overprotective wildebeest.

When she noticed Bruno waiting for more, she added, "Yes, that was the reason."

She slid closer. "I'm already tired of thinking. Overthinking, rather. Can't stand it when I do that."

She shifted nearer, forcing her face not to scrunch up at the twinge of pain that slight movement caused.

Even so, Bruno caught it, opening his mouth to recommend prudence once more no doubt.

She pressed a soft kiss to his mouth before he could protest. It was little more than a feathering of her lips against his. Like the wings of a butterfly landing so briefly their touch could almost be imagined before alighting again.

Still, it was enough to ignite the same fire that was barely restrained inside her.

Surprise lit up his eyes first ... before they smoldered.

When he kissed her back, the light touch of her lips quickly became like a distant memory. All she wanted, all she could think of, was getting more of his lips.

Of *him*.

When he slid his tongue across hers, her body lightened. The heaviness of the constant pain receded to the background.

All she felt was him.

All she wanted.

All she needed.

Everything she'd ever dreamt of in those secret recesses of her being, where she allowed herself to really yearn, her wishes unexamined, uncriticized.

His fingers tangled into her hair, pulling her mouth more fully against his.

Her arms ran along his back. When that wasn't enough, she leaned forward.

"Ow," she whispered against his lips before she could restrain herself.

Immediately, he pulled his mouth away, those

lips just barely beyond her reach. Her gaze dropped to them and she licked her own. Already, she knew he'd be addicting.

"Should we wait?" he whispered so softly that she understood he wanted to as little as she did.

"I can't." After the confession slipped out of her, she realized it was the truth. I mean, she *could*, but it would be torment, and she'd already endured enough of that to last her a lifetime.

She wasn't even embarrassed to fess up to how much she wanted him right then.

His hands moved to either side of her face, forcing her eyes to stare into his. The forest green of his pack magic flashed before he asked, "You promise me that if I'm causing you pain you'll tell me to stop?"

"I promise," she answered right away. Right then she would've promised him whatever he wanted so long as he didn't stop.

"You'll tell me right away, *sí*? You won't let me hurt you." His eyes were so imploring that Naya understood she had to keep this promise. She'd already decided: to hell with the pain, it'd be worth it. But now she saw, plain as day, that it would hurt him if she allowed him to cause her further damage.

She wouldn't do that to him. *Her mate.*

"I promise," she whispered, this time meaning it as fully as he needed her to.

He growled, rough and strong. So masculine that Naya all but felt her toes curl as she leaned into him, silently begging for him to resume where they'd left off.

"Good," he said, just as gruff, just as forcefully, only his touch remained gentle as silk across her skin.

He jumped up from the bed, tugged wide the elastic band of his boxers, and dragged them down. His erection sprang free, and Naya felt herself actually salivate at the sight.

Sister Wolf, the hussy, whimpered inside her, eager for what was to come next even though she'd have to wait for her turn, as Naya already had no doubt she and Bruno would also consummate their bond in wolf form soon. Sister Wolf wouldn't be denied for long.

Bruno stalked to the bed, his eyes illuminated, his gaze predatory.

He guided her down onto her back on the bed, his touch unreasonably ginger when she wanted him to have his way with her already. No part of her cared just then how those injured parts of her would pay the price later.

Later didn't matter. Only now. And how quickly she could get this man—and this fantastically hard and thick erection—as deep inside her as was humanly possible.

He must have read her thoughts across her face, because he said, "We have to take it slow, *amor*. Slow and gentle. But it won't always be that way. We'll do it all. Whatever you want."

She growled like a feral wolf, wrapped her hands around his waist, and yanked him toward her. He stumbled, but caught himself, and she swallowed a twinge of pain like a champ.

"Slowly, my love."

She couldn't do *slowly*. She might never be able to with this man.

She arched up her neck, feeling a tug both at the site of the puncture wound and across her torso, and pressed her lips to his. She licked at his lips until he parted them, until he was growling and panting, as close to losing control as she was.

She spread her legs wide for him as if she'd done this a thousand times before.

He brought both legs between hers as if he'd been doing this with her as many times.

His arms positioned to either side of her so none of his weight spread to her, he kissed her feverishly, intensely, desperately, hard enough that she thought she'd lose her mind and not miss it one bit.

Then he pulled back, his kisses once more the

fluttery touch of a butterfly's wing. He stared down into her eyes, seeming to search for words to say.

She understood. She couldn't think straight any longer. Didn't want to. Didn't need to.

All she needed was lined up to go exactly where she wanted him to.

"My mate," Bruno said as he whispered another kiss across her top lip, then her bottom lip. "The dream I barely allowed myself to have. *Un sueño.*"

Naya nodded, wanting to say the words back, but finding her thoughts a useless muddle. She smiled up at him encouragingly instead, before grunting, Neanderthal-style, and slapping her hands to his ass, and trying to pull him inside her.

His entire body stiffened as he resisted.

She groaned, uncaring that she was sounding like Sister Wolf.

"*No, no, no, mi amor.* Gently. This is your first time. I must be gentle."

"Fuck," she snarled. "I don't want you to be gentle."

He stilled once more, and she figured he'd say something else responsible. That he'd again be the voice of temperance while she was losing her ever-loving mind.

But he didn't.

He stared at her so hard she thought the green

flash of his magic might sizzle deep into her mind, before he growled as low and deep as if his own wolf were riding him as hard as hers was.

As if his desire for her were as primal and real and animalistic as hers.

As if he needed her as completely as she did.

She thought he'd whisper more warnings, more cautions, more beautiful delights she wished her mind were more alert to record for her to replay to herself later.

Again, he didn't.

His jaw hardened and he slid slowly, gently, tenderly ... inside her, every one of his muscles tight as he focused on not hurting her.

His biceps and triceps bulged, the scrawling ink wrapped around his skin dark and bold.

Little by little, inch by inch, he pressed into her ... until finally—*fina-fucking-ly!*—he was buried all the way inside her.

She exhaled deeply and slowly, expanding to accommodate his girth, relaxing her vaginal muscles to allow him to comfortably rest inside her, feeling like everything was right for the first time in longer than she could remember. The sensations were new to her, and she was already fucking addicted. As soon as the tenderness passed in her flesh, she knew she wouldn't be able to hold back.

Here, in the middle of chaos and danger, of possible imminent death, she'd found her mate.

Her center.

Her love.

Already, she could feel her heart burgeoning, expanding to make room for him. To allow for the dreams she'd never dared even whisper aloud.

But here he was. Bruno García Vega.

He'd traveled across the world to find her.

And as he began to move inside her very slowly and very gently, sliding out and then in as carefully as if she were the greatest treasure in the entire world, she whispered, *Te amo*, surprising herself at how easy it was to tell him she loved him. How she hadn't needed to hold back.

She knew he wouldn't hurt her. And he wasn't going anywhere without her.

Mate.

Hers.

She smiled and pulled his mouth down to hers, wrapping her legs around his waist, hissing and groaning in equal measure as he plunged deep inside her.

CHAPTER SEVENTEEN

NAYA

SHE CAME AWAKE, unsure what had drawn her out of a deep slumber. Groggy, she felt as if she could sleep for an entire week and still not feel rested. It had to be all the energy that healing was requiring of her body.

Besides that, she was highly motivated to remain right where she was. Bruno had made their shared time in her bed highly worthwhile, and she was already looking forward to making love with him more—lots more.

Bruno.

She smiled at the thought of him before even opening her eyes. Reaching for him at her side, she found his spot empty but still warm. Then she heard the shower turn on in her bathroom and debated whether she should join him or enjoy a few more moments of indulgent relaxation before their many problems slammed into them with the force of a runaway freight train. No matter how much she wished otherwise, the many complications assailing her were unavoidable. There was nowhere to run or hide anymore where Cassia wouldn't follow.

She stretched until the movement tugged at the long slice across her torso. She still couldn't believe she'd found her mate. There was no denying the truth of that blessing now. Every part of her, inside and out, zinged with excitement. It was the first time since she'd fallen from Shèng Shān Mountain that her attention hadn't immediately gone to her recovering midsection. She was pretty sure Bruno could make her forget her own name with enough time squirreled away with him.

From start to finish, he'd been as gentle with her as he'd promised. And he'd done the same the second and the third time also. She was already craving a fourth round with the handsome shifter who somehow more beautiful inside than he was out.

Light steps trod the stairs up to her porch outside her front door, and Naya scented the air.

Clove.

Her shifter friend would already be able to smell that Naya was in her human form.

Trying to get ahead of her failure to report in

with her, Naya called out before Clove could knock, "Clove, come in. I'm so glad you're here. I've been wanting—"

Clove opened the door with such force that it smacked against the wall as she stood in the doorway, the light of midday framing her slight frame and casting her face in shadow, which proved insufficient to distract from the thunderous slant of her mouth and eyes.

But no, Naya realized, it wasn't as simple as that. Clove wasn't simply angry. A swirl of conflicting emotion looped across her features, as if she couldn't decide what she should feel at seeing Naya again.

Clove stalked toward the bed, where Naya still lay naked beneath the sheets. She stood there for a few seconds, breathing heavily, eyes wild, before she leapt onto the bed, arms wide, slamming into Naya.

Naya winced.

Clove burrowed into her body.

"Ow, ow, ow. Clove. Be careful. That hurts."

Clove eased up, but only fractionally. Not even to relieve the pressure against Naya's ribs.

Naya palmed her small friend on the back. "Lighten up or you're gonna make me vomit from the pain. And you'd better believe I'm gonna point it right at you, since it's gonna be your fault."

At that, Clove pulled out of her fierce embrace,

staring up at Naya as she sprawled, stomach first, onto the comforter. "Are you okay? Did I really hurt you?"

"I'm fine now." Naya hoped so anyway, grimacing as she repositioned her upper body so nothing strained.

"I thought you'd be healed by now. You're a werewolf."

"Yeah, I know. Me too."

"Is something wrong with you? I mean, you know, apart from the obvious?"

"I don't think so..." But Naya couldn't be entirely sure. It was true, she *should* have fully healed by now. It didn't matter that she'd nearly bust in half, preternatural healing could fix anything so long as it wasn't silver poisoning and all the right body parts remained attached.

Clove sat up and smacked Naya on the thigh. Hard. Even through layers of bedding, the slap rang out loudly.

Naya tensed all over as the blow ricocheted up her body. "What the fuck, Clove? I'm hurt here. What the hell are you doing?"

"I'm trying to figure out why the *fuck* my best friend of a million years didn't come find me as soon as she came out of her wolf stupor."

"Clove, seriously? I'm hurt. Obviously, I was

gonna find you as soon as I could, or better yet, ask someone to send for you, since, you know, I'm supposed to be on bed rest. Alpha's orders."

"Mmm-hmmm. So who's in the shower right now? And why do your sheets smell like shmexy times? Like lots and lots of shmexy?"

Naya sighed. "You aren't gonna begrudge your best friend, who very nearly died, like for real, a little celebration time, are you?"

"Helllll no, I'm not. You know me better than that. But how could you do that *before* seeing me? *Me*, Ni? I've been out of my mind freaking out about you! Mav wouldn't let me come along, telling me to stay here and wait like I'm some freaking wolf pet or some shit. And then that hottie rider is all up in here like, 'No, you can't see her, she's resting. She needs to heal-ah.'" Clove wagged her head in mockery while she affected a deep, gravelly voice with a heavy—and highly inaccurate—Spanish accent that sounded more like she was constipated than anything else.

"Well, I have been resting and healing," Naya said. "I only shifted out of my wolf a few hours ago."

"Mmmm-hmmm." This time, Clove sat up and crossed her arms over her chest. "I can tell." Then she tsked and dropped her arms to her lap with a loud thump. "Sisters before misters, Ni. Sisters before misters."

Naya scooted up the bed, propping herself up on a folded pillow. "I know, Clove, really I do. I've thought about you tons since I last saw you."

"Yeah, sure you did." Clove pouted like they were back to being eight-year-olds, when their fights were about so much simpler things, like who got to play with what toy first.

"Clove, *of course* I did. I knew you'd be worried about me, and things have been crazy, and I mean crazy with a capital C. Like top-of-the-line madness. I have so much to tell you."

"But you just had to do some boning before you found me? Knowing I about croaked myself worrying about you? No one would tell me shit about what was happening with you. River and Blake were like dry, shriveled stones." Her voice started out playful and tough, but ended up soft and tender, revealing her true vulnerability. Clove was an only child, and Naya knew she'd long wished Naya were her true sister.

"It's not like that." Naya reached a hand out to Clove, but she didn't take it. "Bruno is..." Naya bit her lip, unsure how it would feel to say the words out loud to her friend. "Bruno's my mate."

Clove went so completely still that Naya didn't even think she was breathing.

"Clove?"

"Wow, that's really great."

"Then why don't you sound like that's really great?"

"I dunno, maybe because you're already leaving me behind. Because already some dude with a dick is your priority over me."

"If you saw his dick, you'd understand. You'd tell me to go have at it as much as I could." Naya chuckled at her attempt to make light of the situation, but Clove, who usually reveled in making raunchy jabs, didn't so much as crack a smile.

"You're breaking all the rules, Ni. Clits before dicks."

Naya frowned, already regretting injecting crassness into their conversation for Clove's sake.

Again, Naya attempted to take Clove's hand, and this time she allowed it, though her fingers were like limp fish in Naya's hold.

"You know I'm not like that. Never have been, never will be."

"Sure, you say that now. But once you get a taste for stiffies, you'll lose sight of your correct priorities real fast."

Naya released Clove's hand and went to cross her arms, felt the soreness in her chest, and fiddled with the sheets at her side instead. "I legit almost just died. *Died*, C. Not just like a fucking exaggeration.

For reals. They didn't think I was coming back. Bruno put his fucking hands inside my fucking ribcage and manually pumped my motherfucking heart to bring me back."

Clove's face paled; no one had told her exactly how bad it had been, that much was clear. She swallowed visibly.

"I almost lost you ... everyone. A cunt of a woman who doesn't deserve to live forever almost took everything I have. So I'm sorry if I didn't hunt you down the second I turned back into myself. I could barely move, C. And that's the honest truth. I woke up and wanted to *live*, really live, before the immortal has the chance to track me down again and do her worst, which is bad as bad gets, trust me on that."

Naya glanced up at Clove again. "And, C, he's my mate. You know better than anyone that I never even let myself hope I'd find my mate. That was like a dream I wasn't allowed to have. So when I found him ... or when he found me, more like..."

"You just had to get his cock inside you."

Naya scowled. "That's what you got out of all that I just told you?"

She sighed loudly, her pixie haircut ruffling with her heavy breath. "No, not really. But it was fun to see you get all riled up." Even after Clove smiled at her with her signature mischief, Naya could tell her best friend only half meant it.

Time would smooth things over between them.

"So." Clove's smile finally transformed into something genuine. "What was it like? Your first time?"

Naya realized she must look like an ingenue, with her flushed cheeks and demure tilt of her head, but she couldn't help herself. Everything about Bruno was dreamy, something she'd never admit to Clove, or she'd really never hear the end of it.

"He was gentle and careful and lovely."

"Gentle, careful, and lovely?" Clove's forehead scrunched up. "Wow. That sounds hot."

"Oh it was, fo sho. It's just that I'm all injured, remember?" Naya waved a hand across her body for emphasis, even though Clove couldn't see beneath the covers. "But it was smoking hot." She sighed, allowing some of that dreaminess to filter through with sudden abandon. "C, I'm not sure I'll ever be able to get enough of that man."

"And his hot rod."

Naya snorted a laugh.

"I told you that you were missing out," Clove said.

"Yeah, well, I had to wait. That was my only option, and I don't regret waiting for a split second now."

"I'll just bet you don't, you naughty thang."

Naya snorted another time. "Not quite, but I'll get there. Of that, I have no doubt."

She hesitated. "C, secret time. You can't tell anyone this."

Clove's eyes widened comically, like secrets were the super-charged, exclusive fuel that sustained her. "Tell me," she barely breathed.

"Bruno waited too."

Clove blinked. "Waited ... for you to heal up some before he jumped your bones? Because yeah, that's what he should do, you doof. Anything less is kinda pervy."

"No, not like that. He *waited*. For me. It was both of our first times."

"Get out."

"Really."

"Fuck, you're serious."

"Yup."

"Girl, you found a unicorn among men. The fucking pot of gold at the end of the rainbow. The fucking leprechaun himself. The—"

"Exaggerate much? It's not like no one waits for their mate anymore."

"Hardly anyone does though. All the dudes in our pack are hornier than ... than ... horn dogs."

"Oh my God, Clove. That's so not true! We have

some really great guys in our pack. Maybe you just *want* them to be horn dogs so you can have at them without remorse."

"Remorse? Why on earth would I have any of that? Aren't you all the girl who wants to live life to the fullest now that you almost died and shit?"

That's when the shower turned off.

"Get out of here, C," Naya said urgently. "Bruno's gonna come out any second."

"And miss congratulating your mate on winning the grand prize? No way."

"Come on. Please?"

"No."

"Pretty please with a red, ripe cherry on top?"

"There you go again, booting me out of your life."

"That's not what—"

"I'm good to talk to while hottie's in the shower. But now that he's coming out, you're all *Scoot, my best friend of forever. I have better things to do.*"

"That's not at all what I'm doing. Is it so much to ask that my new mate not run into my gossiping bestie right after, you know, deflowering me?"

Clove barked a laugh. "Deflowering? Is that what the kids are calling it these days?"

"Seriously, I don't know why I bothered missing you at all. You drive me fucking batty."

"I aim to please." Only Clove didn't, she *really*, really didn't.

The door to the bathroom opened and Bruno emerged, nothing but a towel wrapped around his waist.

And stretches of tanned, firm skin, sculpted, hard muscles, and inky swirls and lines that crossed his arms and chest before scrawling across his hips.

"Yum," Clove said, not even bothering to whisper. "I see why you chose him over me now. I don't blame you anymore. Not one bit. Hey, Bruno? You got a brother?"

Naya would've reprimanded her friend for embarrassing her, but there was never any point. A waste of breath.

Bruno stood still just beyond the bathroom doorway, staring at Clove for a beat. Then his attention slid to Naya and his gaze heated.

"Ni," Clove whispered over her shoulder, which meant she wasn't truly whispering at all. "He's eye fucking you. Just like he did when he first got here. Who woulda thought he'd actually end up really f—"

"Oh-kay," Naya interjected. "I think we get the point. What do you say you leave us the room so Bruno can get dressed?"

"What? And miss the show? Hell no."

"I see nothing has changed with you while we were gone," Bruno said.

Clove glared at him. "Lots has changed, thank you very much. I about died—*died*—I was so worried for my girl here. You know, you could've sent some updates my way. You owed that to me."

"I don't owe you anything."

"I came with you when you went hunting down Naya when she was first taken from here. I helped you."

"You insisted on coming with me even when I would've preferred going alone."

Clove gasped in affront; Naya was certain it had to be an act. With how skilled at offending others Clove was, she didn't take offense easily herself.

"Nothing like—" Clove began, but whatever she'd been about to say, she didn't get the chance to complete it. No great wisdom lost there, Naya figured.

River sauntered through the door that Clove had left wide open. Immediately, his attention tracked Bruno as he pulled a t-shirt over his head. River's eyes blazed pack gold.

"Uh-oh," Clove said, for once mirroring Naya's thoughts exactly.

"What do you think you're doing?" River asked,

his wolf power pulsing through the tension suddenly filling the air.

But Bruno didn't cower at River's power, probably because his own was even stronger. The strength of Bruno's wolf rivaled Maverick's.

"Naya is my mate. We've bonded."

Oh no. That was *not* the thing to tell River.

The Rocky Mountain Pack's beta just stared at Bruno for a few beats. "You don't have Maverick's permission to mate with her."

"I didn't realize I needed it." Though in truth, Naya figured Bruno probably had considered this. Naya wasn't just any shifter. Where Maverick would likely be pleased for any of his wolves to find their mates, she was the exception. As always, the usual rules didn't apply to her. Her future wasn't hers to decide. The wellbeing of all werewolves came before her own happiness.

"But Mav will want me to mate," she told River before she fully decided she wanted to speak up just then, before her full strength was returned. But this was too important to keep silent. "I'm supposed to pass on my genes, remember? So my babies are strong enough to hold the werewolf magic and pass it on too. Mav probably wants me to start popping out babies as soon as possible."

She felt her entire body flush, but couldn't take

the words back. Nothing to scare the bejeezus out of her new mate like talking about having lots and lots of kids after their first date. She hadn't even showered off their first mating, and she was already spewing about babies.

It's not like I want to be a baby-making machine, she wanted to tell Bruno. *It's my duty. Having babies before a hunter or immortal can kill me is pretty much supposed to be my main goal.*

Disturbing as fuck, but pretty much true nonetheless.

But when Naya finally looked at Bruno, he appeared unperturbed. Instead, he continued to stare down River, who was busy staring down Bruno.

"I'll be telling Mav," River said.

"You do that."

"You'll be telling Mav what?" Blake's question trailed ahead of him before he walked through the open door.

"That Bruno here has mated with Naya." River made is sound like a deed punishable by death.

"He did *what*?" Blake asked, voice like the depths of a sandpit. "Without talking to Mav first?"

Bruno sighed loudly. "Maverick is isolated from the rest of us. How am I supposed to talk to him when none of us are supposed to be talking to him?"

"Then you should've waited," Blake said.

"Hey," Naya snapped. "I'm the one who didn't want to wait, okay? And even though you all treat me like I'm some kind of property or problem"—something Naya didn't actually think, but she didn't care just then—"I'm my own person, with my own life. I almost died. Big time. Screw me for wanting to live a little and celebrate the fact that I actually found my mate. Me. When all I'm supposed to be is some kind of freaking pawn in some big game where all were-wolves depend on me." She said that last bit in a whiny, mocking voice. She was well fed up with her fate, dammit!

"Just so we're real clear here. Bruno slept with me in his wolf form until I shifted back to me. He did everything on the up and up. He wanted to wait, I didn't, and you can tell Mav that all you want."

Naya paused, glaring at everyone, even Clove. "Now, I'd like to get dressed in private. I know we wolf shifters have all seen each others' butt cracks, but not today. I want some me time. So you all can excuse me."

No one moved.

"Right now."

River frowned at her. Blake did nothing but stare back, as was his way.

Finally, River said, "Fine, but Mav wants you to go see Scooby to make sure you're all healed."

"Fine," Naya said.

"And after that, we need to talk. So come find me."

"You're right, we do need to talk. I want to know exactly what we're doing to get my sister back."

After some more staring, River spun and left, Blake following a few seconds later, leaving the door gaping open.

"Would it've killed you to close the damn door?" Naya snapped at Clove, directing her frustration at her friend. Nothing like basking in the afterglow of her first lovemaking with her mate with a freaking audience.

Clove ignored her, walking over to her mini kitchen to put on the kettle instead. "I'll wait for you to get dressed, but hurry. We have a lot of catching up to do."

Naya barely managed to swallow a groan. She'd actually meant for Clove to leave as well. She wanted a moment alone with Bruno.

She looked at Bruno, who was already looking at her. He shrugged, like all this had been inevitable.

"Yeah, yeah," Naya muttered, scooting to the end of the bed. Her private time with Bruno was over far too soon.

She'd find a way to slip in more of it though. Guaranteed. She needed more of all that smoking hot goodness. Her attention trailed the length of his body, skimming down strong thighs and calves. She couldn't help but remember how they'd felt pressed against her, and she almost moaned.

Right. She had to clean up, see Scooby, rescue Meiling, save all werewolves. All before mother-fucking breakfast. Or lunch. Whatever.

She blew out a hot breath and slid out from the covers, her naked body fully on display. Bruno's entire body tensed and sizzled as if he'd been struck by lightning. She could actually see his energy crackling and pulsing around his body.

A bright green lit up his eyes and the towel immediately beneath his waist began to tent.

Oh yeah. He was as eager as she was for a repeat.

She smiled coyly, winked at him, and sashayed into the bathroom, wondering if he might throw Clove out just to join her in the shower.

"Clove..." he was saying on a growl as she clicked the door shut behind her. Naya laughed and turned on the shower, waiting for him already.

"...get out."

CHAPTER EIGHTEEN

CASSIA

FOR AN ENTIRE WEEK that felt like twenty, Meiling teetered on the precipice of death. Cassia's team of scientists worked day and night, pumping the girl full of drugs, blood, plasma, and everything else they could think of. They'd resuscitated her from a flatline several times.

Cassia even brought in a mage with a heart as black as his magic. He fueled the girl with spells, amulets, and pulses of his own power, lending her enough fortitude to increase her odds of survival.

Just when Cassia decided it was time to discuss plans with Édouard for retrieving the next of the sisters for another attempt, Meiling's vitals regulated and the team appeared at last hopeful that the girl would survive.

Cassia hurried to the girl's bedside. Her blond

hair was dark with a week's worth of sweat, her complexion wan. The girl hadn't opened her eyes but for a few feverish moments days before.

Tubes and cords snaked from her to machines that beeped and beat out a steady rhythm.

She was alive.

Davina had lasted less than an hour before her heart gave out, and no amount of electroshock was able to revive her.

But Meiling lived.

"How is she?" Cassia asked Hodges, the scientist studying machine readouts and jotting the results on a clipboard before also transferring them to a tablet. Those who worked for her weren't allowed mistakes, so they'd developed redundant systematics.

The man, whose hair was nearly as heavy with sweat as Meiling's, despite the cool temperatures of the lab, met her waiting stare, but she could tell it took determination on his part not to cower.

Good. Fear was healthy.

"She's gotten past the worst of things. Every sign indicates that she'll continue to improve now. Of course, your immortality magic is unprecedented, and we have no surefire way of anticipating everything that might happen."

"No need for disclaimers, Hodges. Tell me what I need to know."

He nodded sharply; a bead of sweat broke free and trickled down the side of his face.

"Her bodily systems are operating normally now, though she is still recovering. Her cognitive functions are normal, though she hasn't woken up in days. However, everything indicates that she'll make a full recovery. Her pupils are responsive, everything is working as if she were a patient well on her way to recovering from some grave illness."

"Your prognosis?"

"In another week, she'll be fully stable. She'll be weakened, but her readouts will be steady."

"How long until you can administer the solution that will disconnect her shifting ability from the moon?"

Cassia listened to every report her team gave her. She absorbed the nature of the proprietary formula they'd developed that would allow Meiling's werewolf genetics to mimic those of an ordinary wolf shifter. Cassia didn't, however, retain much of that information. She understood magic far better than she did science. Magic made sense. It was how everything in nature worked. All of life ebbed and flowed, continually seeking balance. In nature, things lived and died, progeny continuing on to complete the cycle anew. Cold and heat balanced each other as well as dark and light, night and day, fast and slow.

Power was ultimately nothing more than energy, and energy never disappeared, it only dissipated and redistributed. Even how she rode the air wasn't as much magic as it was an application of her understanding of how energy worked. The elements were energy.

"I believe that it would be best to wait at least a month before administering the genetic alteration," Hodges said.

Cassia frowned. "A month? From now, or from last week?"

"From now."

"And is this your conclusion or the team's?"

At this, Hodges hesitated, casting nervous glances at the other whitecoats buzzing around the room, keeping busy now that their mistress was there, scrutinizing their every move.

"The team's. We've discussed it, and we believe that in order to increase the chances that the girl's system will accept the genetic mutation, it's best to wait."

"I see. And what do you think will happen if you administer your solution today?"

He startled, a shiver jerking his body. "Today? As in right now?"

"Yes."

Édouard walked slowly until he stood between

Cassia and Hodges. It was endearing how he always wanted to protect her, even when she was fully capable of defending herself, especially from a mere human.

"I ... well, it's possible the girl could handle the transformation without a hitch—but it's not likely. Her body's already undergone intense shock from assimilating your magic."

"But she *could* survive the additional change."

"Of course she *could*. But the longer we give her to build strength, the better odds that everything will proceed smoothly."

"I can bolster her strength with magic."

"Um, well, that might help, but..."

"Speak freely."

"The mage, he makes us all uncomfortable. We're not sure what he's doing, and it doesn't always seem like he has the patient's best interest at heart."

Cassia thought it was more likely that Kirill's heart was a shriveled husk that barely managed to pump blood through his veins. If he weren't so eager to do whatever she asked without question, she wouldn't use him. But he never disclosed what he did for her either. She'd worked with him for decades and never once had she caught rumor of what he did for her circulating through the magical communities. The man spoke in the language of money, power, and fear, and that was a language she spoke fluently.

"Your concern is noted," Cassia told Hodges, who nodded curtly. "Any other reason why we shouldn't proceed today?"

Hodges cast a panicked glance at his teammates, but none of them came to his rescue, busying themselves with their readouts and inspections with renewed vigor.

Hodges cleared his throat. "You asked us to monitor her. Our job has not only been to ensure she survives, but also to make sure the immortality magic mixes well with wolf magic."

"And...?"

"It's just, well, in order to properly study her, we need to allow her to reach a baseline, something she hasn't achieved yet. We have her pre-immortality readouts of course, but we need her to fully stabilize so we can accurately analyze her progress. To truly understand how she is processing your magic."

Cassia took a seat in an armchair at the head of Meiling's bed and crossed her long, shapely legs at the knee. "I'm not interested in analysis, only results. If you adjust her shifting abilities today, then we'll see results much faster. We'll know soon whether the two types of magic are compatible."

"Yes, but only to a certain extent—"

"If you're worried about me surviving, remember that I cannot be killed. The prudence and delay are only to make sure the experience I will have as both immortal and wolf is a pleasant one. No one wants the wolf inside me to be tormented and driving me toward instability. My responsibility as an immortal is to be strong, healthy, and balanced."

"Yes, of course," Hodges said too quickly. Cassia didn't miss the nervous twitch of his cheek that suggested he didn't entirely agree with her. Perhaps the human considered her imbalanced? How dare he? Once he'd served his purpose, she'd kill him first.

Cassia studied Meiling. The girl was wholly unmoving. But a machine broadcast her heartbeat aloud to the room. It was steady. Her breathing was normal. Her brain function was normal.

Cassia stood, causing Hodges to jump again. She smiled at him, doing nothing to hide her wicked delight at finding him so on edge.

"You have two weeks. If everything proceeds as expected, in two weeks you'll alter her shifting capabilities."

Hodges gazed at the floor, clutching his clipboard and tablet against his chest like a shield. "Yes, ma'am."

Cassia studied the rest of the team Édouard had handpicked, noting how not a single one of them would meet her waiting gaze. Half of the team was absent, likely resting in their quarters until their next shift.

"You are the leading minds of your respective fields," she said. "I know you'll achieve what we've set out to do. And then your families will be rewarded beyond your wildest dreams."

That part was all true. Cassia would throw money at their families to such a degree that they wouldn't miss the men and women Cassia would have to kill.

She couldn't trust them with her secrets. They knew too much of the magical world, and they were too powerful in their knowledge of how to make alterations to it. Their deaths were unavoidable, but their families would be set for life, and then for many generations afterward. One sacrifice for the well-being of many.

"Two weeks, that's all you get," she called over her shoulder before she exited the lab and took to the skies right away, needing to discharge her nerves and impatience.

Success was so close she could taste it.

CHAPTER NINETEEN

MEILING

"I'M SORRY," breathed the woman in the white lab coat with the compassionate, conflicted eyes and the long shiny hair, too softly for anyone to overhear, not even the vampires stationed at the corners of the room surveilling her every move. A second later, the woman injected some clear unknown substance into Meiling's IV line, then made note on a clipboard.

Meiling steeled herself for the pain that would inevitably arrive next, snaking through her veins like a viper, usually delivered without apology or warning. Experience told her she had a few minutes at most before she'd be wishing for relief more than she'd ever wished for anything in her life.

She'd thought the torment from the silver had been bad, the way she'd endured its effects for days, her skin feeling like it was disintegrating under the constant contact. But that had been before all this.

She'd been at this place, wherever and whatever it was, for days now, so many that she'd lost count—it had been several weeks at least. All she knew for certain was that Cassia had breathed into her mouth, giving her what seemed like the reverse of the kiss of death she was notorious for, and was directing whatever experiments a whole team of men and women in lab coats were performing. Meiling was the lucky chosen one to be the lab rat. And whatever they were doing felt incredibly, incredibly wrong.

So far, Meiling had only seen two rooms and many ceilings as she was once transported across the facility. For three long, interminable days, she'd remained within that first room, which had turned out to be lined with thick, unbreakable plastic windows, through which the creepy immortal watched her for hours on end. And then continued watching while her wolf paced the small cell, throwing herself against the walls, snarling and snapping, trying to antagonize Cassia enough for the immortal to enter the room to face her like a true, honorable opponent.

Only, Cassia obviously didn't care about honor or what was right or moral. She hadn't fallen for Meiling's lure, instead choosing to be a voyeur for the entire three nights Meiling was in the moon's thrall. Though the immortal could have certainly made the view one-way only, she'd kept a light on above her head. A wholly vicious and satisfied smile had marred her otherwise impassive face.

Whatever the immortal wanted with her, Meiling *couldn't* give it to her. She had to find the way to resist. She couldn't let her win, no matter what.

Since the full moon waned and Meiling returned to her human form, she'd been in this one room. Its colors were muted, the bed upon which she lay cushioned. The lighting soft except for when one of the lab coats pinned a spotlight on her veins to draw blood. Once, they'd flipped her on her back and injected a needle into her spine. That had been fun.

The constant *beep, beep, beep* of machinery set at low volume, and her terrified thoughts, were the only company she had across the days and nights.

She sucked in a rapid breath at the first burn within her veins. Then she forced herself to breathe calmly, deeply, so she could survive this next wave of torture. Her only goal was to get to the other side of this nightmare, one way or another. It was all about conserving as much energy and mental ease as she could.

Her breath hitched, but she forced it to continue

along evenly. Her back arched; she pressed it down fully against the narrow bed, but didn't manage to actually relax before fire raced through her insides.

She gulped uselessly, clenched then opened her eyes, tightened her fingers, and wished with all her might that she could tear through the many restraints that held her down, all laced with silver, and kill every single last one of these *cào nǐ mā*. Even the kindly lab coat who smiled at her before carving out her insides with a dull knife. She knew a hundred ways at least to kill them all in under a minute. All she needed was one chance. One mistake.

But the silver threads woven through her ties were enough to weaken her, if not to burn through to her bones. And whatever was running through this IV managed to subdue her the rest of the way.

"Clear," someone yelled, and Meiling shoved down the sob that bubbled up in her chest.

She would *not* show a single one of these assholes how much they were hurting her. She'd survived vampire masters who were as cruel as Cassia. She could get through anything so long as her mind held on—

Two cold metal paddles pressed against her exposed chest, pushing the electricity through her body. This time, there was no stopping her back from arching off the bed with the tension of every single one of her muscles clamping painfully.

The power surge dragged on and on before it finally ceased, and she slammed down against the bed, suddenly relaxed all over, like she'd never move again.

"Again," the same man called, and she wished she could focus so she could figure out which lab coat it was and take her time making him pay later.

"Clear," he bit out another time, shoving the two metal paddles above her naked breasts again.

This time, as her back arched, her head pressed painfully back against the bed, shaking, her every thought and fear and hope rattling free as if she'd never catch up to them again.

She ground her teeth, peed into the catheter, and clenched her toes, pressing them against the bed so her legs arched too.

The shock lasted longer this time. When it finally eased, something worse happened.

Her bones, ligaments, and skin began to stretch and tear the way it did when...

No, it wasn't possible. Had a full moon cycle passed with her in here? Had she lost that much time to their draconian experiments?

"Get the silver bands off her," someone shouted. "Leave only the leather and plastic."

Fingers scratched and tugged at her skin, releasing some pressure, only to have more bands tighten against her.

When her jaw lengthened, she had no doubt. She was on her way to becoming a wolf. Again.

Too soon.

It was all bad. Wrong. A sin against her nature.

The familiar cracks, pops, and breaks underway, Meiling knew of nothing else to do but give into the shift.

"Now," the same man ordered. "Shoot the sedative."

When darts stung her morphing flesh, only then did she realize that the IV, catheter, and all the other many tubes and cables attached to her would have sprung free.

Another few pinches. One dart hit her in the neck, another in the thigh. She lost track of all the rest.

If they knocked her out before she completed her shift yet again, that wouldn't be good for her wolf. *You can't halt a natural process like this, it might damage it*, she wanted to yell at the bastards who'd stolen her free will and were busy raping it.

She feared if she spoke she'd accidentally bite off her tongue with all her unwilling thrashing, so she did all she could think to do. She reached out to

Sister Wolf with all the reserves of will she had left, urging her to complete the shift as quickly as possible. She surrendered her humanity, laying the woman upon a sacrificial altar for the whole's greater good.

Cào. *Come on, Sister Wolf*, she thought. *Pull through this.*

Then she thought no more.

CHAPTER TWENTY

CASSIA

AT THE TWO-WEEK MARK, Meiling had made impressive progress. She'd been strong enough to receive the gene alteration her team had developed. Whether it had been the girl's natural resilience, or a combination of the scientists' concoctions along with Kirill's spells, Cassia didn't know. She also didn't care.

Again, the girl's body had fought the new adjustments. She clung to the veil that separated life from death by nothing more than a stray thread. And yet again she returned from the edge of the cliff, once more stabilizing.

But it had taken her another couple of weeks for the team to become certain the girl would survive, another two weeks during which Cassia thought she might crawl out of her skin and be done with all the waiting already.

But the moment of victory had finally arrived. Cassia was salivating as if a seven-course meal of entirely new flavors were laid out before her, or as if a brand new lover waited for her sprawled naked on a bed, one as experienced as she was in the arts of seduction and pleasure.

"Mistress appears excited," Édouard said as he walked beside Cassia, and she couldn't remember if he'd ever made such a personal comment to her before. But his voice thrummed with a shared enthusiasm, as if he were actually ... happy ... for her.

So she allowed his lapse of place. "I am, Éd. These are breakthrough times."

"Quite." He held the door to the lab open for her and she walked in, blinking against the sudden dimness, but not waiting for her eyes to adjust before moving to the back, Meiling's home for the last five weeks.

This time, the entire team was assembled and waiting for her. Six bright lab coats, six clipboards clutched in front of their bodies, and an array of nervous, tight smiles that didn't illuminate anyone's eyes.

"Is she ready?" Cassia asked the group as one.

A woman stepped forward. "She's as ready as our medicine can make her." Doctor Patel was young, with long hair as dark and lustrous as Cassia's. She was the only one Cassia wished she didn't have to kill. The woman was sharp enough to be considered a genius, and ambitious enough to excel in a field dominated by men, two qualities Cassia couldn't help but admire.

"The patient has only woken twice," Doctor Patel continued, "but each time we were able to instigate her shift."

"And how did you do this?"

"By causing pain. It seems the fastest way to get her to shift against her will."

Another reason Cassia was partial to the female doctor. She didn't so much as blink in discomfort at any of their tactics. Perhaps Cassia could find a way to keep her on. Once Cassia achieved becoming a wolf shifter in her immortal body, she was sure she could imagine some other project Doctor Patel would excel at.

"Very good," Cassia said. "The plan remains as before?"

"It does. We'll electroshock her until the pain causes her to awaken and shift, then she'll infect you with what is now wolf shifter magic by scratching you, passing it on in the way of werewolves. The science suggests that though the subject is now essentially a wolf shifter in nature, she is still capable of passing on her magic by infection via a scratch or bite. You should immediately become infected, and, unlike with werewolves, you won't have to wait until the next full moon to undergo your first shift. You'll be capable of transforming immediately, with control and without pain."

Cassia licked her lips hungrily. "Excellent." After all this time, it was finally happening. After a thousand years, she was on the verge of a radical change in experience. She could barely begin to anticipate what it would feel like after all these centuries of sameness. There were only so many new external experiences a person could go through before the stimuli dulled to nothing.

"Let's begin immediately."

Cassia had given some forethought to what might happen if she were unable to control her wolf at first, but in the end there was no one more powerful than she; no one would be able to restrain her. And she wasn't about to lock herself up in a prison laced with silver. While it would contain her—maybe—she didn't trust anyone to have that kind of power over her, not even Édouard.

No, they'd all just have to hope that Cassia could control herself as a new wolf. It was the only way.

Doctor Patel was the only one not to hesitate,

complying immediately. The others, led by Hodges, scampered behind her, flipping switches, adjusting dials, and taking notes on their clipboards before they all turned expectant faces toward Cassia.

"You should position yourself within easy reach of her hand that will more or less become her paw," Doctor Patel said. "The shifts haven't lasted more than a few seconds so far."

Cassia stood at Meiling's bedside, while Édouard picked up the armchair and positioned it directly behind her, ever anticipating her needs. Ordinarily, Cassia would object to Édouard behaving as if she might become infirm. But she might soon be quite grateful for a chair to plop into.

Cassia peered down at Meiling, at the face so familiar to her. She'd examined it so often over the twenty-two years the girls had lived. All those years checking in on them, waiting for them to mature, studying their habits and their movements, ever hoping they'd become the kind of creatures needed to withstand the vastness of immortality ... all distilled down to this one moment.

With her eyes closed, Meiling appeared peaceful, as if she were simply sleeping.

"Do it," Cassia said, and Doctor Patel called out, "Clear," and slammed matching defibrillator paddles onto Meiling's nude chest.

The girl's body jumped, arching off the bed as if seized by an invisible force from above.

Her eyes popped open, and, unseeing, looked straight at Cassia. Their clouded crystalline blue burned with an otherworldly, milky brightness.

Then, as they all watched, fur burst forth from her flesh. Bones crunched as they snapped. She crumpled and deformed into a gnarled and twisted mess of body parts until, just as quickly, she reassembled into a large, majestic wolf that strained against the restraints carefully wrapped around her to contain her even in her new shape.

"Now," Doctor Patel said, and Hodges and another white-coat grabbed one of Meiling's front paws and extended it toward Cassia.

She brought her forearm beneath the massive paw and the doctors gouged her flesh with the wolf's claws.

Blood pooled from the wounds, three parallel lines that cut nearly to bone. It stung like a mother-fucker. And yet Cassia couldn't keep from smiling.

She felt the magic, foreign from her own, working within her.

She was a wolf shifter. The beast she'd dreamt of being already howled and sang and fought to be released from inside her, yearning to discover itself, to understand this new infinitely powerful creature, this eternal form of animal perfection.

While Meiling's wolf collapsed and crumpled and reassembled once more into the naked body of a young woman, Cassia stepped off to the side, away from the scientists, vampires, and machinery.

She closed her eyes, blocking out all distractions, and then reached for the wolf inside her and ... tugged on her, willing her to take over her body.

In a painless instant, Cassia was a wolf.

She shouldn't have been as shocked as she was. After all, Cassia was a master of magic and energy, and the wolf inside her was nothing more than manifestations of both.

And yet, her surprise beat through her with as much force as the strength of the wolf that was now hers. She wanted nothing more than to tear out of the lab and run into the woods, sprinting in a body made for running, for prowling, for chasing and hunting. For dominating.

But before Cassia could do anything beyond register her success, Meiling arched off the bed once more, this time on her own, no electrical motivation needed.

She roared, and though she was a human once more, she sounded like an enraged wolf. Like a furious beast capable of snapping any restraint in half.

Before she had time to process what was needed, Cassia's wolf tucked itself back inside her body, and Cassia discovered herself standing in a pool of her shredded clothing.

Breasts pressing into Meiling's shoulder, Cassia leaned over her, intending to perform the kiss of death as she'd done hundreds of times before—this time, with the addition of recovering her immortality magic.

But Meiling thrashed and jerked her head with such power that, even when Cassia pushed both hands against either side of her head, she struggled to keep her still long enough. Digging her fingers into Meiling's skull so hard that she scored her skin, she slammed her mouth against Meiling's.

She sucked in Meiling's breath, using it to transfer the girl's life force—and also the immortality magic—to mingle with her own, making Cassia even stronger.

But when Cassia pulled with her breath, Meiling yanked back.

Cassia's eyes opened wide as she felt their breaths tangle before the energy of each went in the opposite direction it was supposed to.

Cassia could no longer discern up from down,

inside from out, or who or what she was for several terrifying moments, and after a dizzying swirl, when her back smacked into the medical bed, she stared up into eyes that were no longer her own.

But should have been.

Absolutely should have been!

Unblinking, unmoving, barely breathing now that her mouth was no longer pressed to Meiling's, she met violet eyes so unique she'd recognize them anywhere.

How many times had she studied their unusual shade in the mirror?

In her bastard of a father?

More than enough times to be certain that something had gone terribly, terribly wrong.

CHAPTER TWENTY-ONE

BRUNO

AS IF SHE'D been drowning and finally managed to break the water's surface, Naya became alert all at once with a shuddering twitch and gut-wrenching, guttural gasp. Asleep at her side, an arm draped across her nude body, Bruno startled and rolled off the bed, immediately lowering into a crouch, hands up in front of his chest, ready to attack. Adrenaline thumped through his body, making his limbs uncomfortably shaky as he cleared the vestiges of sleep.

"What is it?" he asked urgently, his voice still thick. "What's wrong?"

He swept his sharp shifter sight across the dark planes of Naya's cabin. He saw nothing, not even in the shadowed corners. Felt and scented no one. Not even the curtains fluttered.

"Naya," he prompted as he flung open the door

to the bathroom and swung around to inspect the small kitchenette, before dipping to check under the bed. He didn't expect to find anything, but with a treasure as precious as his mate, he couldn't be too careful.

Naya pushed up to sit, dragging herself up so she could lean against the headboard. Her heart beat too quickly, and he could smell her fear, when, in the weeks he'd known her, he'd never experienced her to be frightened of a single thing. Not even when that *puta* of an immortal was hunting her down like prey.

Certain that whatever threatened her wasn't inside the cabin with them, he sat on the bed next to her, running a soothing hand along her legs.

"*¿Qué pasa, amor?* What's happening?"

Instead of looking at him, she stared straight ahead into nothingness. Her eyes were unfocused, her breathing too fast considering they'd been asleep for hours, and he'd made sure she'd been well spent before they drifted off to sleep. He couldn't seem to keep his hands off her now that she was his.

"*¿Peligrosa?*" he asked, softly this time. "Are you hurting?"

For several long seconds, she didn't respond. He prepared to beg her to tell him what was happening so he could help her, but then she shook her head, her long silken hair sliding delicately across those strong beautiful naked shoulders of hers.

His touch became softer still as it slid up to caress her thigh. "Tell me."

Now she nodded, pulling in deep, calming breaths, though her heart continued to race. Its panic was so loud to Bruno's ears, it was as if a drummer were playing directly beside them.

"Something's wrong with Meiling," Naya said in a sudden rush. "I don't know what's going on, but I can feel it. Something bad's happening to her, Bruno. We have to find her. We have to help."

He sighed silently, yet still heavily. "You know we've been searching for her nonstop since she disappeared, *amor*. There's been no sign of her."

"She didn't *disappear*," Naya snapped, though he understood her frustration wasn't directed at him. "That..." She gritted her teeth for a moment as if no insult were sufficient. "That motherfucking asshole bitch of a woman took her. Snatched her out from right under our noses. As if Meiling is nothing more than a fucking plaything to her, to do whatever she wants with."

Bruno tucked a strand of hair behind her ear. "I know, *Peligrosa*. I realize how difficult this must be for you..."

"You didn't see what she did, Bruno. She

exploded a fucking centuries-old vamp just because she could. She relished in causing him pain. She played it up for her fucking audience, as if torturing a man and then exploding him from the inside out were fun and games."

Quiet, he waited.

"The mack-daddy of all the vamps was scared of her, actually scared, and he looked like he ate humans for breakfast, lunch, and dinner, then picked his teeth with his long-ass disgusting nails."

Naya breathed in and out, her chest deflating, heartbeat slowing. She cast her eyes down and away from his; instantly, he wished for her to look at him again. "I fucking *hate* that she's stuck with that horrible woman and I can't do anything about it."

"I know." Meiling's predicament weighed on him too. He scooted farther onto the bed, running both hands through his hair, pulling on it. "We're out of leads though. Mav's called in every favor, every connection."

"Then we'll have to find more to call on. More people to ask."

"We've asked—"

"And we'll ask again and again until we get results. I am *not* losing my sister when I only just found her. Besides, she's an heir to the bloodline just as much as I am. All werewolves—hell, all wolf shifters in the world—should be looking for her high and low. She's the most important thing now."

He smiled a bit sadly. "She's not more important to me than you."

Finally, she met his waiting gaze again. "I won't be able to live with myself if something happens to her while I could have done something to help her. And..." Another slow cycle of breaths. "I'm afraid something already has. I don't know what I felt, but it was enough to scare the crap out of me. It's like she's calling to me ... or something, I don't know. Like I'm linked to her, at least a little bit. This whole twin thing's so new to me, but don't twins all over say they feel each other?"

"I think so."

"I mean, I never felt her before." She chuckled darkly. "I didn't even know she existed. But now that I do, I can't help feeling ... I don't know. Dammit, Bruno, I don't fucking know! But something yanked me out of a deep sleep, and it wasn't roses and rainbows."

She paused, and her eyes burned into his so intently he realized he'd do absolutely anything she wished of him. He'd scour the damn surface of Earth to find Meiling and return her to his mate.

"Cassia's got her, and she's hurting her. We have to find Meiling now. Right the fuck now." Then, in a soft voice that betrayed her fear: "Or it might be too late."

Bruno rubbed his face, glancing toward the window. It was dark out, not yet dawn. Wolf shifters slept erratic hours. Their wolf sides preferred the night, but their humans preferred the day. That meant that in a pack someone was always awake. It was never fully still or quiet.

But since Naya had recovered enough that it was certain she'd resume a normal life, together, they'd followed up every lead they could find. Maverick had forbidden her from leaving their territory, concerned for her safety now more than ever, but that hadn't stopped Naya from making calls and a thousand internet searches, from scouring the entire Rocky Mountain Pack territory for any sign of her sister, though he guessed that was as much to burn off nervous energy as it was a hope of finding a needle in a haystack.

They'd last seen Meiling in China. For all they knew, she was still at the Shèng Shān Monastery. It was the likeliest option, really. It would have been easy enough for the immortal to imprison her there after capturing her. The vampire masters had built a cell there that would hold a werewolf, even when she was in her animal form.

"I have to convince Mav to take me back to the monastery," she said, as if reading his very thoughts.

"You know he won't agree to that. You've tried already." *Mierda*, had she ever. Naya was *persistent* and then some. It seemed almost every day she hounded the beta or gamma into asking Maverick, who was still isolating himself from Naya for her safety, if they could plan a rescue mission.

Maverick's answer was always the same: *Not yet.*

He wouldn't endanger the pack, along with the one heir to "the Oak" MacLeod's nearly extinct bloodline that was safe, to take on a mission they had no guarantee of completing.

The terrain that surrounded the monastery, and especially the tall peak it stood upon, provided an impregnable defense. Plus, the monastery was filled with highly skilled and trained fighters, many of whom were ancient vampires. The older a vampire, the greater their strength and magic.

Besides, there was no confirmation that Meiling or the immortal was even there anymore. If anything, the only useful rumblings that had returned to them from so much net-casting was that the immortal's jet had taken off shortly after theirs. Mordecai's divination via runes had confirmed this. According to the wizard, Meiling was with Cassia, but not where they thought they were. He couldn't discern anything more specific about her whereabouts.

This was enough for Maverick to continually deny Naya's requests for a rescue mission. The risk was too great, their information too sparse, and the only direct answers they had—*sí*, from a mage—suggested that the invasion of a highly fortified fortress filled with brutal warriors would be a fool's errand.

Even Bruno, who'd never trusted a mage of any sort a day in his life, had seen enough of the strange wizard brothers to place his faith in their guidance.

And Naya knew all this. They'd talked it out perhaps a hundred times over.

None of it, however, tamped down her desperate need to do something, anything, to deliver Meiling back where she belonged. With her. At her side.

Safe.

So Bruno suggested one of the only two things that seemed to soothe her ragged nerves lately. "Shall we spar, then?" The tightness of her shoulders and press of her scowl were too ferocious for lovemaking to force her mind off Meiling. He smiled at her; she was even more striking to him for her fierce loyalty. "I believe I owe you some payback after last night."

The more desperate she became, and the more helplessness she experienced, the more devastatingly efficient and brutal she was in the ring. He was no slouch in a fight, but more often than not she'd been getting the drop on him. He suspected she'd begun picturing him as Cassia.

"Yeah," she said, nodding distractedly. "A good fight is exactly what I need."

And after that, a long shower, he thought, and again she'd be open to lovemaking, when they could lose each other in their embrace, in pleasure, and, for at least a little while, forget there were beings in this world as heartless and ruthless as Cassia. When he was inside her, as deeply as possible, when they became one, it was the only time she was unable to think of anything else.

Once more he'd deliver her from her worries, enmesh their hearts, bodies, and souls so profoundly that neither of them could deny that magic was real, capable of surprising miracles. Together, entwined in one another, they'd find hope. Time and time again.

But first they'd fight.

Bruno smiled, mischief twinkling across his gaze. "Hurry up, slowpoke. I'm going to beat you this time."

When her responding smile seemed to wipe the worry from her face, his heart lightened. She slid from the bed, padding over to the dresser and bending over to remove yet another set of workout clothes. He didn't bother to hide his appreciation of her naked form. Of the round curve of her ass that literally made his mouth water. She was perfection inside and out. Everything his heart and body needed. Already, his dick twitched in anticipation of what would come later, when they finally collapsed into bed together, tangling themselves up in blissful oblivion.

He leapt from the bed, slapped her on the ass, and danced out of the way when she squealed and raced after him. He was determined to give her the spar of her life.

He vowed to give her all of himself in every moment.

That still didn't mean he'd beat her, despite what he'd said. She was lightning fast, more determined than seemed possible, and wily. She'd kick his ass, flip him over, and ride him, all in the same night, just as savagely.

She was true perfection.

And she was all his.

Tonight and always.

With a spreading grin, he watched her dress, delighting in every stretch of skin, muscle, and curve.

"Hurry up already," he said, though she was dressing faster than he was. "I'm ready for my prize."

That would always be her.

He beat her out the door of her cabin, racing her all the way to the training complex. He arrived first, but just by seconds, and her narrow-eyed look told him he'd pay for it on the mat.

He couldn't fucking wait.

CHAPTER TWENTY-TWO

CASSIA

MEILING'S EERIE VIOLET EYES—*HER* eyes—
blinked groggily back at her, as if the girl were having
as much difficulty making sense of whatever had
passed between them as Cassia was.

It should have been a simple retrieval of her
immortality magic. Out of necessity, Cassia had
shared a small portion of her eternal life with Meiling. She had to, of course, ensure that it was possible
for a person to survive the unlikely combination of
wolf and immortality magic. Such a pairing didn't
exist in nature. Cassia couldn't take the risk of
trying out wolf magic without first being certain
that the mixture was survivable. It became a logical
and crucial step of her experimental process,
decided on long before she'd even followed Brighid
and Aiden O'Connor into that pub and secured

their agreement to bring children into the world on her behalf.

The next step was supposed to be the easiest one yet: Cassia was to reclaim what belonged to her. Her immortality magic was to be hers alone. That had always been the plan.

What had gone wrong? She'd performed her kiss of death a thousand times. Granted, she'd never actually lent her immortality magic to anyone, but the logistics behind the process were the same. *Should* have been the same.

And yet ... if Cassia was staring up into her own eyes, was Meiling looking down into her own? Or had Cassia somehow duplicated herself? Were there now two of her?

Cassia's long black hair tumbled across Meiling's bare shoulder, the braid thick and shiny. It was as if Cassia were studying herself in the mirror. She'd rarely met a man she couldn't sway to do her bidding with a few silly flutters of her eyelashes, pouting lips, and sashay of her hips. They were fools who thought only with their dicks, almost all of them.

Meiling couldn't have both her immortality magic *and* her looks.

Cassia could sense the bit of her magic that hadn't returned to her as planned, alive and thriving inside the girl.

She snarled up at her.

"Mistress?" Édouard said uncertainly. "Uh, what should I do?"

Edouard hadn't sounded this uncertain in at least a hundred years, since that time she decided to confront Cyrus about his reckless ways and ended up spread into a million fragments.

But not dead. Never dead.

It had been, however, excruciating as she endured her body piecing itself back together from infinitesimal fragments after Cyrus had blown her up in a surprise bomb of his own devising.

Decades later, she'd made him—cautiously—an ally. Decisive attack without hesitation was a valuable trait. And the man had never been bothered with such problematic qualities as mercy.

"Something went wrong," Cassia said without looking at her most trusted servant. "I'm the one lying on the table now."

She could actually hear the shock and doubt circling the room across her vampires and scientists. A ferocious snarl and glare would have done wonders to whip them in place, but Meiling's eyes had cleared of their hesitant confusion, and now Cassia could almost see the thoughts racing across them, plotting her attack—and likely escape.

That wasn't going to happen—though Cassia was

now the one in straps, Meiling completely free and poised above her.

"Quickly, grab her and don't let her escape," Cassia ordered to the many guards she had stationed throughout the room.

But no one jumped to fulfill her command.

"Now!" she bit out.

"Ah, Mistress...?" Édouard began, sounding as weak and useless as he had when she'd first found him, a strung-out, newly turned vampire hunting on the streets of sixteenth century Paris. "How can we be sure it's you?"

As if feeling her window of escape closing, Meiling hopped off the bed. Her knees wobbled, and she collapsed to all fours. But in the next moment she was up, looking frantically at all the people standing between her and the single door out of there.

Cassia's thoughts raced, searching for the fastest solution. In words as biting and rapid as the shots from a machine gun, she spit out, "When I found you, you'd just drained two children, a girl and a boy, paupers. They're names were Auberta and Gre—"

"Grenier," he finished in a tormented whisper.

Meiling lunged for the door, knocking into Hodges and another of the doctors. Useless, they bowled over, crashing into two of her vampire minions aiming to intervene.

"Take her down," Édouard commanded the other vampires in a harsh growl, proving that all the time she'd dedicated to shaping him had been worthwhile. "Don't let her leave!" To the scientists, he snapped, "Get my mistress out of those restraints right this second."

Doctor Patel and two other white coats jumped at the uncommon sternness of his voice, then rushed the bed, hastily shoving their omnipresent clipboards aside, shifting equipment, removing wires and tubes that slunk everywhere like snakes before reaching for the looping bindings.

Meiling crouched and took the brunt of impact from one vampire on a shoulder, before flipping him over her body. He landed with a clang of metal trays and tools.

A second of her minions charged her, a blur of inhuman speed, this time managing to tackle her to the floor. She landed hard with a whoosh of air, but was back on her feet too quickly, given that she was still unsteady, struggling to maintain her balance. Whatever sedatives and drugs Cassia's team had injected her with continued to burden her reactions.

The same vampire spun, grabbed both of Meiling's legs, and yanked her back down. Next, he climbed her body in a flash, too fast for even Cassia's eyes to register, then bit down on her neck.

With a snarling scream, Meiling tore him off her; he took a chunk of her flesh with him, blood dripping down his chin.

The girl sprinted for the closed door—in Cassia's body. With her hand on the handle, the vampire, licking her blood from his lips, clutched her shoulders from behind and tugged her downward. She resisted, dragging him with her as she wrenched the door open a few inches.

She was uncommonly strong. Unusually resilient. Determined. Her instinct to survive strong.

Too bad she had to die. Perhaps this one would have served her well.

Three more minions and Édouard latched on to the girl—but by then Cassia was free.

While the five vampires held Meiling down, Cassia swooped between them, clutched her head, and twisted in one loud satisfying snap.

"Back away," Cassia said, breathless, the chaos exciting her. As the vampires gave her room, and Édouard moved backward in a bow, Cassia added, "It will take her at least half an hour to recover. Her spine is completely severed."

Cassia could narrow down the timeframe quite precisely. Her revolving-door of scientists had worked on many projects for her over the years, including cataloging how long it took werewolves and wolf shifters to heal from an itemized list of injuries. If she was anything, Cassia was thorough—another reason she would live for millennia after all the vampires and humans in that room had decayed to nothing but dust.

She wanted to kill the girl, of course. But she wouldn't take the chance.

Whatever had passed between them, it shouldn't have.

Cassia longed to retrieve that small part of her immortality magic. It wasn't Meiling's to keep, even in her death, and it wasn't enough to keep her alive when her end arrived. It was no more than Cassia had given Davina, and the girl was colder and deader than a coffin itself.

Cassia also longed for the return of her familiar physical form. But again, she wouldn't risk it.

Were she to perform another reversal of her usual kiss of death, *si*, she might get the fragment of her magic *and* her body back—or something worse and equally unpredictable might happen.

No, it wasn't worth it. Cassia could live in the body of this girl. It was a fine specimen. Strong, agile, limber, and possibly as appealing as her own. Cassia could apply her gift of seduction as easily through this shape. And who knew? Perhaps she'd learn to enjoy the change after all this time. Not having to stare at her reflection and see constant evidence of her father. With their shared violet eyes gone, Cassia could perhaps finally finish putting the man and the enormity of his betrayal behind her.

At long last, perhaps she'd be free of him.

She'd be *free*.

Smiling at the prospect, she rolled her neck around her shoulders, becoming acquainted with this new body, and as she did she felt all eyes in the room on her. Where they belonged.

She narrowed her attention onto her servant, the one whose teeth were still stained pink with Meiling's blood. What had been *her* blood until not that long ago.

"You," she said in a voice that sounded both like hers and Meiling's at once, though it was pitched with the unmistakable power that was all her own.

The vampire startled and stiffened. Now that she was a wolf shifter—a glorious wolf shifter; she grinned wickedly—she could scent his fear permeating in the sparking air.

"You drank from her without my permission."

"You ... you told us to attack."

"*No*, my faithful servant, Édouard, told you to *take her down*."

"I-I took her down, Great Immortal, as ordered."

He bowed low as if that single gesture could erase his previous disobedience.

Idiot, she snarled, barely keeping the thought to herself.

She stalked toward him, closing the distance far more slowly than was necessary, reveling in how each of her light footfalls made him twitch and tense all over again.

When her nose nearly pressed against his, when his objective beauty in that marble-like face blurred away, she whispered in a seductive roll that was more lethal than a silver blade pressed to his heart. "You *fed*."

Too late, he cast his eyes downward in submission.

"Without my permission," she added. "Without my leave."

He opened his mouth, likely to protest, though he must already realize it was futile.

She didn't let him speak. "You only exist to please me. I am immortal. You are fleeting. Nothing more significant than a speck of dust, blowing in the wind across a vast empty space."

He glanced up at her quickly before once more dipping his head low.

"You are insignificant. I am everything. When I bought you, your purpose was to serve me and fulfill my every wish. You have betrayed me. You followed your own direction instead of mine."

"I'm sorry, Mistress," he rushed to say, but the title sounded foul on his lips. Édouard was the only one who called her that in a way that didn't make her stomach clench.

Bored with him already, she pounced without warning, gripping his head between her hands with such force that not even his vampire strength would move him.

Oh, she was liking this body just fine. If only it had occurred to her before. She was benefiting from the decades of complete dedication Meiling gave to honing her body into a weapon, and without any of the effort. *This* was the way to go. Perhaps she should figure out how she'd managed this body swap after all. It might serve her again when she grew tired of this body.

Pressing her lips to the vampire's, she didn't bother to enjoy their fullness or softness, too excited to draw his life force in to fuel hers.

She sucked in his breath, his very existence; it filled her like a warm beverage, tingling all the way down, reminding her she was invincible, in whatever shape she chose to take.

Another gloriously satisfying kiss of death completed, Cassia pulled back, releasing the vampire's head. He crumpled to the floor in a spent heap, knocking into the foot of the bed with a hollow thud. The other vampires jumped away from him as if he were contagious—all but Édouard, who gazed at her in adoration, much as he always had.

She licked her lips, a slow tantalizing roll, and chuckled when half her minions followed the path of her tongue, seemingly aroused by her. Her power. The other half appeared ready to piss themselves, a result that was equally satisfying.

She peered at her team of scientists huddled together on one side of the room. They stared at her, their expressions locked into varying states of terror, and possibly admiration. Doctor Patel was the only one not to seem ready to bolt if she were to give them the chance—because none of them were idiotic enough to do something significant without her express permission.

She took in Édouard, and as she did he dipped his head in respect.

"How may I serve, Mistress?"

Ah, if only she had a dozen of him, life would be so much more pleasurable.

"Kill the girl and dispose of her body." She paused. "Actually, no, give her corpse to the team. They can experiment on her." Glancing at the PhDs, she added, "Study every single thing you can about her. What happened once her wolf was disconnected to the moon, when she received my immortality magic, when we swapped bodies. Search for any physical sign of any of these instances." She smiled again. "Oh, and besides all the usual studying of a shifter, look for any ties between her and her sisters. See if there is actually some sort of bond between identical children."

Careful to hide her regret, she swallowed. How had she not thought to do that with Davina's body? Instead, she'd handed the body over to Davina's alpha in an effort to keep the peace. She frowned at the sudden bitterness tingeing her tongue. It was a mistake she wouldn't commit again.

"Everything proceeds as discussed until I return," she told Édouard, who knew not to inquire about her plans. He knew as much and as little as she wanted him to.

Then, with nothing more than a mental caress of the wolf inside her, she thought, *Shift*, and in an instant she stood on four paws, feeling the strength, freedom, and vitality of her beast thrumming inside her.

Her vision was different as she scanned the room a final time. It was as if she could actually see the energy of the beings inside it, could feel them as prey or predator, and sync herself up to their rhythms, the beating of the organs inside them for easy and efficient attack. She could hear their breathing, their hearts, their stomachs growling and churning. She could smell their fear, thick as it permeated the room.

She grinned a wolfish smile, and one of the white coats, a young doctor by the name of Todd Spakerton, leaked several drops of urine. She must be as terrifying as she felt. Even Édouard appeared afraid of her.

All the decades of planning and inconvenience, every step and life she'd set in motion, they were all worth it. Life had never felt so rich, so vibrant, so ... exciting.

She had no doubt her first kill in this form would perhaps be even more satisfying than her kiss of death. Would she also absorb her kill's life force, or would she simply end a life as a wolf? That was an unknown no amount of research could resolve. She was one of a kind. The only immortal-wolf-shifter in existence.

She had to know.

Once more, she swept across the room those eyes that seemed more like some sort of infrared scope than eyeballs. All the bodies vibrated with pulses of energy.

Not bothering to mull her decision over, she lunged for Hodges. She'd never liked him much, though he'd served his purpose well. As tall as his ribs, she closed the space between them and snapped her teeth around his throat. As she ripped his throat out over his surprised squeal and then gurgle of his blood, she focused on envisioning herself sucking out his life force, much as she did with her kiss.

And it worked.

Cazzo, it motherfucking worked.

She spat his throat and gristle to the floor. His body fell into the rest of her staff behind him. Each and every one of them was appropriately terrified.

Good, the fresh reminders always served to keep them in line. She had no more long-time projects for them—yet. She would. She'd always dream. She was a visionary. She'd soon decide on the next step in her evolution, and they'd do their part to see it through.

Next, she jumped over Meiling's still body, shrouded in Cassia's past, and padded toward the door. Almost closed, she pawed at it, realizing she'd have to remember to secure her exit from situations more carefully than she did in human form.

One of her minions sped in a blur to open the door wide for her. Head held high, she stalked through the threshold, every bit the predator. He zipped ahead, yanking wide the door to the laboratory.

Beyond lay every one of her immediate dreams

come true. The forest spanned far and wide at the edge of her estate. She'd run, she'd hunt, she'd sniff all the scents and fresh air. She'd mainline the raw power of nature.

Tasting victory, she sprang forward, clearing the door with grace and elegance, every one of her muscles functioning optimally.

Every single sacrifice was worth it.

Scenting a rabbit that had already discovered her and was hopping away, she sought out her next prey. This one, she'd gobble right up.

Her wolfish smile wide, she bounded away, lighter than she'd felt since her sisters' deaths, what felt like eons ago.

CHAPTER TWENTY-THREE

MEILING

A LOUD CLATTER and then a sharp hiss startled her to alertness with a soft, pained groan that another timely bang concealed.

Thank the holy book, she thought as her eyes adjusted to the bright lighting directly overhead. One of the lab coats was bent over, scrambling to pick up a metal tray and the medical tools that used to be carefully laid out on it, now spread across the cool tile, smeared with traces of blood, but nerves made his fingers loose as noodles. A metal clamp scooted across the floor, skittering away from his erring touch.

She was still in the room she'd been in for the last many days, but she now lay at the foot of the bed with its silver-woven shackles.

Cassia was gone, as were the vampires, save for her number-one slave, Édouard. With a scowl of disapproval tightening his otherwise unremarkable face, he leaned imperiously over the panicked doctor, who was crawling around to pick up all the implements the man and the rest of the team had used to ruin her.

Four other men and women in white coats looked on, half shooting the object of Édouard's attention sympathetic grimaces, the other half not seeming to care at all. The doctors were all human; they had to have turned off all compassion to work for someone like Cassia. Even the woman with the glossy dark hair, who'd occasionally shot her kind smiles, hadn't hesitated to poke and prod her at the immortal's command.

Édouard held a short sword in one hand, the blade gleaming beneath the harsh lights, no longer dim like they'd been before, when the scientists had pretended she was a patient instead of an unwilling lab monkey—dispensable. The soft, calming music was gone, all other efforts toward a soothing ambience discarded.

She winced at the soreness in her neck, significant enough to almost tug her back down into the blackness, but she was mindful not to make a sound. For once, good fortune was on her side. No one had noticed her yet, all their attention turned to the lab coat's noisy, hapless distraction. But the medical bed would only hide her from view for so long.

She doubted the gangly vampire who should have *Yes, Mistress* tattooed across his forehead—as if a bloodthirsty, vicious immortal without a conscience deserved respect!—carried an unsheathed sword to dispatch the doctors. The blade was surely silver. She was certain the weapon was intended for her.

That shrew Cassia had gotten what she wanted, so now she'd ordered her done away with as if she were nothing but refuse. And what had Cassia gotten from her? Meiling tried to remember, but the thoughts eluded her. Acid churned suddenly in her gut. The immortal had said she was going to suck back out her immortality magic, and then ... something had gone wrong. She had ended up staring down at her own face. Had Cassia duplicated her? Was Cassia now walking around in a body just like hers? Like Naya's? Had she managed to retrieve the immortality magic from her?

No, she decided after a moment. It was still there. That part of her that now felt foreign, as if it didn't belong.

Meiling could not—would not—allow the woman to continue prowling the earth. She was its greatest predator, the most dangerous threat, and yet she was a secret in the shadows that could strike at any moment. That *would*.

Meiling anticipated Édouard's movement a fraction of a second before he spun to look at her, as if he'd sensed something was off. She could feel his stare glued to her even as she forced her eyes softly closed, making her body limp, her breathing deep and constant in the calm rhythm of someone unaware that she was two strides away from being a body and a head—but no longer together in one whole.

Seconds mattered now. The obsequious vampire servant was undoubtedly competent for Cassia to trust him as she did. He'd carry out her orders soon, and Meiling still wasn't convinced she could defend herself with the severity of the pain running up and down her spine. What the hell had happened to her? Did the shrew actually try to yank her head off her shoulders? By the holy book, it felt as if Cassia had almost made off with her head.

Meiling waited longer than she wanted to, but only when she no longer felt the heat of the vampire's gaze did she peek her eyes open. The servant was turned around once more, barking orders at the doctors, especially the clumsy one who now stood, tray and its accoutrements trembling in unsteady hands.

This was her chance, likely her only chance. Nothing stood between her and that silver blade but a swing of the vampire's arm.

Her back and neck muscles stiff as a tree trunk beneath the pain, she longed to stretch, to roll her head around her neck to test her mobility. But any unnecessary movements would give away her only advantage: the element of surprise. They thought she was still out cold on the floor. But she was a werewolf —or something—she no longer felt the constant connection to the moon, a sensation so continuous throughout her life that she hadn't realized it was there until it wasn't. Now she yearned for that connectedness as if it were a missing organ. She could, however, still feel Sister Wolf inside. And something else too. Different magic. A power that felt like ... Cassia.

Her lip curled involuntarily, but she rushed her thoughts along. If not for the knocked-over tray, her head might have been sliced off already, her heart carved out while she was still unconscious. He would have been thorough, and either of the steps was all but guaranteed to end a wolf shifter of any sort— linked to the moon or not.

It was now or never.

As quietly as she could, straddling the line between swiftness and stealth, she slid more fully behind the medical bed and its solid base, careful that her naked flesh didn't squeak against the tiles beneath her. Without a pause, she crouched, fought the wave of dizziness that surged up through her neck before rushing down her spine with unpleasant warmth, then peeked around the side of the bed's base.

One of the lab coats was staring straight at her, eyes wide, his mouth opening already.

She lunged toward Édouard as the scientist rose an arm to point in her direction, ramming her shoulder into the vampire's waist.

But he'd reacted quickly, and was half spun around to face her when she slammed into him. Together, they crashed into doctors and equipment on rolling wheels with a cacophony that hurt her ears.

But Édouard didn't drop the sword.

While she fought back darkness clouding the edges of her vision—that impact hadn't done her pain levels any favors—he clamped one arm around her, holding her tightly on top of him, and sliced down with the blade, cutting into her back as she rolled out of the way a moment too late.

Blinking away the unconsciousness attempting to lure her back to it like a siren's song, she stepped to the right, wobbled, then to the left, stumbled—

Édouard thrust forward, slashing at the space she'd only just occupied.

Dizzy, she was one wrong move away from blacking out. Fresh blood oozed down her back. But if she was grateful to the wicked vampire masters of the monastery for anything, it was for pushing her far past her limits. They'd beaten the notions of weakness and surrender out of her long before she hit puberty. She was used to barreling through her perceived walls head on; hell, it was expected of her, every damn day.

As Édouard lunged sword first, she spun inside his hold, pressing her body against his chest before shooting a fast elbow into the artery running under his armpit. As the weapon fell from his grip, she snatched his arm, rammed her butt into his waist, and launched him over her head. The instant he landed, she was on top of him, her hands gripped to either side of his head. With a loud, satisfying *snap*, she twisted his cranium from his shoulders.

He went limp beneath her. She breathed a single inhale of relief before: "Watch out!"

It was the raven-haired woman with the somber eyes.

Fumble Fingers was full of surprises. The tray once more at his feet in another mess of parts, he clutched the sword out toward Meiling.

A flash of regret swam through her that the man should choose monsters over her, murderers over their victims. But she didn't let it slow her down.

In one rapid scan of the room, she spotted the defibrillator on a table next to the bed. Still plugged in. A green light suggesting they were charged and ready to go, no doubt with the intention to torture her some more.

Surging upward, in one smooth move she spun and looped both hands through the handles. When she turned again, she didn't pause before kicking the sword from the man's hand and slamming the paddles against his only sizable patch of exposed flesh, his cheeks—and pushing the button.

His entire body shook forcefully, his eyes rolling into the back of his head.

Payback, asshole.

Like a domino, he fell back into the others, who jumped out of the way so as not to touch his still-electrified body.

She snatched up the blade, straddled Édouard where he lay on the floor, and set to carving out his heart. As he would have done with her, she'd rip out his heart, sever his head from his body, then burn the whole mess, just to make sure he wouldn't be coming back for another stage of undeadness.

But with his suit jacket cast aside, his shirt ripped

open, and the silver blade carving a hole around his heart, charring his pale flesh as it went, she stilled. Her shoulder muscles tensed, sending a spike of fresh pain up her neck.

She didn't know how it was possible, but she sensed Cassia. The immortal was nearby, heading toward them quickly. She wasn't in the mood to be Cassia's plaything any longer. Neither was she strong enough to confront her, who was theoretically unkillable.

Using up a final second, with a flick of her wrist Meiling completely severed Édouard's heart from the many arteries keeping it in place. She then pulled the sword free, yanked the door open, and ran without so much as a glance back at the stunned scientists.

The next room was long and narrow, equipment of all sorts on counters, wedged between several coolers filled with tall, narrow glass tubes. She sped past it all—until she caught a reflection of herself in one of the large windows.

She tripped over her own bare feet, catching herself before falling, and turned to stare.

Not at herself.

Not at the woman she knew herself to be. Not at the sister who looked exactly like Naya.

But at the immortal.

Meiling looked precisely like Cassia. Not a single hair was different.

Panic bursting inside her like another surge of electricity, she shook the terrifying discovery loose and commanded her legs to move.

Out the door. Away from this place. Far from the immortal, who looked like her now.

She'd figure it all out later.

There was only one thought: *Get free*.

Clear of the laboratory, she emerged into an inner courtyard that seemed serene with its tended garden beds and classical buildings enclosing it on all sides.

Get off the property, was her next thought.

And once she did, she tossed the sword at the base of a tree in a thick forest, and ran as fast as she could, hoping she was moving toward a city.

If the immortal looked like her, Meiling had to get to Naya before Cassia did, before the immortal could deceive Naya into thinking she was Meiling, getting past her guard before Naya realized who she actually was. Cassia would cut her down.

But Meiling had no idea where she was, what continent even. She had no money, no skills to navigate this world so foreign to her. It wasn't as if life as a warrior monk in a vampire-filled monastery had prepared her for the ways of modern living.

Even if she could steal a mobile phone as people had now, and she figured out how to use it, she'd have no way of reaching Naya. She couldn't just ask humans to look up the number for a pack of wolf shifters. And how exactly would she find supernaturals to ask? If she did, how could she trust them? How would she know they didn't work for Cassia, whose web would surely stretch wide, especially around her property?

No, the only way for now was on foot, out of sight. If she wasn't on the same continent as Naya, she'd figure it out soon enough, and then she'd squirrel onto a plane as she'd done before, when she'd first learned of Naya's existence and set off to warn her, what felt like ages ago.

Cassia was almost at the laboratory. The certainty hit her like a rock to the forehead, shot at her with a slingshot.

She and the immortal were linked somehow.

If Meiling sensed Cassia's movements, was the reverse also true?

One problem at a time. She'd take this challenge on in bite-sized pieces or she'd make no progress at all, overwhelmed by panic and helplessness.

Run, run, run. That was all that mattered.

Meiling reached for her Sister Wolf for the first time in her life. Never before had she been within, just waiting for Meiling to let her loose. The full moon had always been the one to free her.

And as Meiling's body—now looking like Cassia —stretched and shifted in mid-step into that of a large, sleek, and powerful wolf, Meiling trained her focus on one single imperative: *Find Naya. Save my sister.*

CHAPTER TWENTY-FOUR

CASSIA

SHE'D ONLY JUST BEGUN TASTING the power of being a wolf—agile, deeply attuned to her natural surroundings, impossibly fast, light, strong, and brutal—when her intuition screamed a warning. Running through the forest that surrounded her estate, the wind in her fur, she skittered to a quick stop, wondering at the cause of this sudden bad feeling.

There was no one left in this world she loved, so it wasn't that. Her sisters and mother were long gone, their smiles a vague, hazy image in the dusty corners of her memory.

Édouard was the closest she had to a friend, but the vampire was fully capable of dispatching an unconscious wolf shifter, no matter how many hours

Meiling had spent training under the pompous ass that was Ji-Hun.

She took a few more steps, intending to ignore the niggling feeling. But, again, her intuition twisted her gut.

Cazzo! she thought as she turned around and sprinted back in the direction of her estate. After how hard she'd worked to secure her beast, she should have been allowed to enjoy it. But *no*, people were always working to interfere with her plans and disturb her.

Her muscles elongating, her paws skimming the earth, every movement effortless and seemingly divine, it took her mere minutes to arrive back at her lab. The door hung ajar, so she slipped inside in her wolf form. As she entered the inner room, she froze for a moment before commanding her body to shift back into that of a woman.

Édouard lay dead on the floor next to the medical bed, a gaping hole carved out around his heart, still in his chest, her stupid scientists standing around staring at him, wiping their asses with their many degrees instead of putting them to good use.

"What happened?" she snarled at them, doing nothing to conceal her disgust. How many times had they disappointed her? How many more times would she allow it?

"The girl healed more quickly than we expect-ed," Doctor Patel said, her ever-present clipboard glaringly absent this time, her brows drawn low over troubled eyes. "She attacked Édouard before any of us realized she was awake. It shouldn't have been possible. It was too fast, fifteen minutes instead of thirty. No one heals that quickly from a severed spine, not when she was already unconscious."

Cassia pressed her lips together as she slid Édouard's head onto her lap, cradling it atop her legs. That was probably the effect of her immortality magic. But she'd given the girl so very little of it, just a taste, the minimum amount necessary to verify that Cassia's power could mix with wolf shifter magic and not kill its host. Nothing more. It shouldn't have been enough to double her healing time. What happened here should have been impossible.

"You should have anticipated how my magic would affect hers," she hissed into the room. Her team, Doctor Patel included, took a step back from her until their backs pressed against each other or the wall. "That's what I pay you for. That's what I protect your families for."

Édouard's eyes were empty and glassed over as he stared up at nothing. Her heart grew heavier than usual. She shook her head. Meiling ... she'd kill the girl twice over for what she'd done.

A large smudge of hastily mopped-up blood was all that was left of Hodges. Another thinner, fresh trail of crimson splattered near Édouard's body.

Cassia pinned Doctor Patel in a stare. "Did he hurt her before she killed him?"

The woman's throat bobbed before she answered. "He sliced her back open with his sword."

"And that blade was pure silver," she thought aloud. At least the wound wouldn't heal easily for the *puttana* of a foolish girl. That was something.

"Tha—"

Cassia whipped her head down toward Édouard at the sound of his strangled voice, which wouldn't have been recognizable as him if not for the fact that she'd spent centuries in his company.

"Oh my God, he's alive," one of the idiot doctors said from the other side of the room. The team couldn't even tell when someone was dead. She'd kill them all before the day was over. *Useless, overpaid morons.*

Blocking them out, she lowered her face to Édouard's. "I'm here, Éd. I'm here."

"Than—" His breath hitched. He tried again. "Thank ... you."

Her heart twisted into a dozen tangles.

"You ... saved ... me. When I was ... lost ... you saved me."

He choked and gurgled, eyes drooping.

She brushed his thin, fine hair, like an infant's, from his forehead. He was too far gone for her to save him with anything less than her immortality magic. For good reason, before Davina and Meiling, she'd never shared it with anyone. It was hers to wield and use, and hers alone. Power diluted was power wasted. And after what had happened with Meiling, whatever had caused them to swap bodies, Cassia especially couldn't risk getting stuck in a body as frail and pathetic as the vampire's.

His eyelids fluttered open drunkenly, his words so soft that if not for her newfound animal hearing, she might have missed them.

"*Merci...*" He wheezed, a single breath rattling through his chest as if it were hollow. "My mistress..."

His eyes closed heavily, his body relaxed, and what strength he'd had to hold on left him entirely, along with whatever it was vampires had that made them live on even when their hearts no longer beat.

She stared at him for several long seconds that drew out into a minute. All around her, the silence was heavy, oppressive, swimming with her team's fear.

When she had no doubt his pale, sunken cheeks would haunt her for years, she slid out from under him, allowing his head to fall to the floor unceremoniously. His neck twisted at an inhuman angle, suggesting Meiling had broken it before killing him ... before carving out his fucking heart.

Now, her favorite servant of centuries was nothing more than an empty shell. He'd soon disintegrate into nothing. She'd have to train a whole new vampire to serve her, and with the sampling of useless creatures she'd been buying recently, the prospect wasn't promising.

Glancing up at the many humans in white coats, several of them startled. One squeaked like a frail mouse, another urinated in his pants again, something she could scent thanks to her wolf senses.

"You failed me," she said in slow, halting words. Doctor Patel, closest to the door, bolted from the room; the others remained pinned in place, as if paralyzed.

She'd allow the woman doctor to live long enough to think she had a chance. At least Doctor Patel had some gumption instead of standing around like the others, waiting for her next move, easy pickings.

Though perhaps it was simply that they acknowledged how far superior she was to them. They hadn't a single chance at escaping the fate she dictated for them.

Calmly, she held the eyes of the first as she

walked slowly toward him. She clasped her hands to either side of his head and kissed him, sweeping her tongue across his—and tasting his fear—before sucking out every drop of his life force.

As she did, she registered the frantic sounds of the others scrambling to exit the room. She didn't care. She'd catch them all too easily. Humans were boring prey, unable to put up a fight. And their life force was ... lacking. There was no magic, no exquisite power, to commingle with her own.

But their life energy was a sweet elixir, she admitted to herself, like the energy drinks the humans were so fond of. She'd get a jolt of strength that would last her at least a week.

Besides, she was hungry. Thirsty. Ready for more.

She pulled her lips away from the man's, licking hers before he fell inelegantly to the floor and onto her feet. Frowning, she kicked him off her, turning to the now empty room.

She took a final glance at the vampire who'd been with her for so many of the recent years, and at how his skin had already turned pasty, taking on a marble hue, his essence draining rapidly from him. Before long, he'd deflate, sinking in on himself. Sighing heavily, she shook her head in lament, blond strands bouncing everywhere, temporarily startling her. She'd have to get used to this new body that looked so unlike her. Pulling the door wide, she walked through, pausing only once she emerged into the sunshine and the empty courtyard.

She'd shift to hunt down the rest of her team. Then she'd rid herself of the other vampires who'd done nothing to save the only one of them who'd mattered to her at all.

After that, she'd leave it all behind.

She'd hunt down Meiling. She'd make her pay for Édouard's death.

Oh, would the girl ever pay. She'd taken her only companion from her? Well, Cassia would take anyone who'd ever laid eyes on her. She'd already killed Li Kāng and Davina. Next, she'd track down Naya and kill her while Meiling watched. Then she'd take out the entire Rocky Mountain Pack. She'd wipe out every single stupid wolf shifter who'd ever felt a thing for Naya. After that, Lara was only a short flight away. After Meiling watched her kill the alpha, ridding the world of the entire line of supposed heirs to Callan "the Oak" MacLeod's bloodline, she'd take her time killing off the Andes Mountain Pack.

They'd all pay. She wouldn't stop until they had.

It was her new purpose, her new mission, and she

allowed it to roll and expand through her until it filled every little crevice.

She was immortal. She was wolf.

She was all powerful.

No one would dare stop her. No one would manage it even if they tried.

With all those kisses of death, and with her wolf, she'd become more powerful than all the other immortals walking this world combined.

As she felt her power surge inside her, she threw her head back and laughed, an airy delight that hadn't slipped from her lips in perhaps a decade.

Was that Meiling she felt? Yes, she believed it was.

Cassia's immortality magic knew that the small bit that remained in Meiling was *hers*. It linked them together.

The girl was moving fast. Running toward her sister, no doubt, thinking there was a chance she could save her.

Cassia laughed again. They were in Southern France, and Naya was in the Western United States. And Meiling knew nothing of modern life and how it worked. Ji-Hun had prepared the girl for combat alone, and had otherwise left her understanding of modern workings sometime in the Dark Ages.

A plan blossomed within Cassia. She'd follow the

girl, who was unaware Cassia could track her with the ease of a homing beacon. Then she'd lay her trap, and only when the two sisters stood well within it, would she spring it.

Her wolf was ready for the hunt.

Her heart was ready for vengeance.

She'd have both. She'd have everything she deserved.

Tilting her head into the air, she sniffed, scenting one of the doctors off in the direction of the parked cars.

With a grin that spread to tighten her face, she called on her wolf, transformed in mid-leap, and charged.

Rocky Mountain Pack
Book Four
Wolf Destinies

Continue the explosive adventure with Naya, Bruno, and Cassia in **WOLF DESTINIES**, the next book in the Rocky Mountain Pack series.

BOOKS BY LUCÍA ASHTA

~ FANTASY & PARANORMAL BOOKS ~

WITCHING WORLD UNIVERSE

Magical Enforcers
Voice of Treason
(coming soon)

Magical Dragons Academy
Fae Rider
(coming soon)

Six Shooter and a Shifter
When the Moon Shines
When the Sun Burns
When the Dust Settles

Rocky Mountain Pack
Wolf Bonds
Wolf Lies
Wolf Honor
Wolf Destinies

Smoky Mountain Pack
Forged Wolf
Beta Wolf
Blood Wolf

Witches of Gales Haven
Perfect Pending
Magical Mayhem
Charmed Caper
Smexy Shenanigans
Homecoming Hijinks
Pesky Potions

Magical Creatures Academy
Night Shifter
Lion Shifter
Mage Shifter
Power Streak
Power Pendant
Power Shifter
Power Strike

Sirangel

Siren Magic

Angel Magic

Fusion Magic

Magical Arts Academy

First Spell

Winged Pursuit

Unexpected Agents

Improbable Ally

Questionable Rescue

Sorcerers' Web

Ghostly Return

Transformations

Castle's Curse

Spirited Escape

Dragon's Fury

Magic Ignites

Powers Unleashed

Witching World

Magic Awakens

The Five-Petal Knot

The Merqueen

The Ginger Cat

The Scarlet Dragon

Spirit of the Spell

Mermagic

Light Warriors
Beyond Sedona
Beyond Prophecy
Beyond Amber
Beyond Arnaka

PLANET ORIGINS UNIVERSE

Dragon Force
Invisible Born
Invisible Bound
Invisible Rider

Planet Origins
Planet Origins
Original Elements
Holographic Princess
Purple Worlds
Mowab Rider
Planet Sand
Holographic Convergence

OTHER WORLDS

Supernatural Bounty Hunter

(co-authored with Leia Stone)

Magic Bite

Magic Sight

Magic Touch

STANDALONES

Huntress of the Unseen

A Betrayal of Time

Whispers of Pachamama

Daughter of the Wind

The Unkillable Killer

Immortalium

~ ROMANCE BOOKS ~

Remembering Him

A Betrayal of Time

ACKNOWLEDGMENTS

I'd write no matter what, because telling stories is a passion, but the following people make creating worlds (and life) a joy. I'm eternally grateful for the support of my beloved, James, my mother, Elsa, and my three daughters, Catia, Sonia, and Nadia. They've always believed in me, even before I published a single word. They help me see the magic in the world around me, and more importantly, within.

I'm thankful for every single one of you who've reached out to tell me that one of my stories touched you in one way or another, made you laugh or cry, or kept you up long past your bedtime. You've given me additional reason to keep writing.

My thanks also go to my reader group and advance reader team. Your constant enthusiasm for my books makes every moment spent on my stories all that much more rewarding.

And a special thank you to Mayu for answering my questions as I dreamed up Seimei Do. I'm grateful for your gentle guidance.

ABOUT THE AUTHOR

Lucía Ashta is the Amazon top 20 bestselling author of young adult, new adult, and adult fantasy and paranormal fiction, including the series *Smoky Mountain Pack, Witches of Gales Haven, Magical Creatures Academy, Witching World, Dragon Force,* and *Supernatural Bounty Hunter.*

She is also the author of contemporary romance books.

When Lucía isn't writing, she's reading, painting, or adventuring. Magical fantasy is her favorite, but the romance and quirky characters are what keep her hooked on books.

A former attorney and architect, she's an Argentinian-American author who lives in North Carolina's Smoky Mountains with her family. She published her first story (about an unusual Cockatoo) at the age of eight, and she's been at it ever since.

Sign up for Lucía's newsletter:
https://www.subscribepage.com/LuciaAshta

Hang out with her:
https://www.facebook.com/groups/LuciaAshta

Connect with her online:
LuciaAshta.com
AuthorLuciaAshta@gmail.com

facebook.com/authorluciaashta
bookbub.com/authors/lucia-ashta
amazon.com/author/luciaashta
instagram.com/luciaashta

Printed in Great Britain
by Amazon